Dear

& hope

you enjoy!

Peggy Krause
Wild Beau and Her Kittens

Peggy

ISBN: 1-4636-9211-0
ISBN-13: 9781463692117

Dedication:

I dedicate my humane Kitty Tales Trilogy to all the people in the world who champion and advocate for animals, whether by doing TNRs of feral cats or trying to domesticate them, building enriching retirement sanctuaries for the primates who were tortured for years in medical research facilities, protesting the animal entertainment industries, volunteering at animal shelters, and everything else they do to help the helpless. Please keep up this most noble of work.

To my gifted illustrator, Christian J. Pogorzelski— Thank you for all your wonderful ideas and creativity. Thank you for your incredible talent and your invaluable input. And thanks for all the laughs.

Table of Contents

OTHER BOOKS BY PEGGY KRAUSE:

"Finding My Molly"—First book in The Kitty Tales Trilogy—On the National Humane Education Society's recommended reading list!

"The Scruffy Little Crumb-Grabbers"—Second book in the Trilogy—Winner of the National Indie Excellence Finalist Book Award!

Chapter 1
Missing Ferdinand

It was very late on a hot summer night and Soupy, the cat, was sleeping snugly next to his seven-year-old owner, Molly Taylor. Molly's bedroom window was open to welcome in any breeze that might blow by. The garbage cans had been put out by the curb for the garbage collector in the morning. Soupy awoke to a clanging noise.

What was that? He quickly looked around the room.

He heard the clanging noise again coming from outside. He jumped off Molly's bed to investigate. Soupy felt it was his job to protect his family as best he could. He ran to the window, jumped up on the windowsill, and peered out onto the street. He saw that the source of the noise was only a small raccoon who had pushed the lid off of the garbage can to look for something to eat. This made him think of his foster son, Ferdinand. Soupy had gotten lost last summer and ended up living in a hollow log in the forest preserve for a few months. Shortly after getting lost, Soupy had found a tiny, hungry orphaned raccoon. He immediately adopted the baby, named him Ferdinand, and took care of him until he grew old enough to take care of himself.

Soupy loved Ferdinand with all his heart and missed him very much. He sat on the windowsill wistfully watching the raccoon pick through the garbage, until it scurried away with a large piece of pizza that Molly had only taken one bite out of at dinner that day. Soupy hoped the little raccoon enjoyed his pizza. He pressed his forehead against the screen window and watched the raccoon scurry down the street until he couldn't see him any longer. Soupy sighed heavily.

I wish I could see my son again.

He hopped down from the windowsill and jumped back onto the bed. He curled up into a ball next to the back of Molly's neck. She smiled a little in her sleep. Soupy fell asleep a few minutes later and dreamed of his beloved son.

❊ ❊ ❊

The next day, all of Soupy's cat friends, Lola, Lila, Puff Puff, and Spider Man, gathered on his porch for a visit.

"Hi, guys," said Soupy from inside the screen window. He wasn't allowed to go outside like his friends were.

"Hi, Soup," answered Spider Man.

Spider Man was a very chubby boy because his owner, Marcy, spoiled him with delicious treats all the time. But if anyone mentioned Spider Man's weight to Marcy, she would shake her head and insist that "He's not overweight; he's just a little husky."

"Hi, Soupy," said Lila and Lola in unison.

Lila and Lola were all black cats who lived to-gether with Cindy and Steve, an attractive couple in their mid-thirties. The girls' house was right next door to Soupy on the south side. But the color of Lila and Lola's fur was the only thing that was simi-lar about them. Lila was the oldest of all the cats and the wisest. She was beautiful, having a black coat that was very sleek and shiny, and she *knew* it.

Lola, on the other hand, was the youngest of all the cats and was smaller than Lila, slightly pudgy, and her coat was a little on the dull side. But little Lola was adorable in her own right and simply a joy to know.

"Hi," said Puff Puff, the tiniest cat of the group. Puff Puff was an all white, long-haired fluff-ball of a cat. He was also very timid for some reason. The other cats often wondered if he had acquired his name because he looked like a powder puff or be-cause he *acted* like one. But he was a very sweet boy and his friends loved him just the way he was.

Lila noticed that Soupy looked a little down-hearted.

"What's wrong, Soupy?"

Soupy looked at Lila. "Oh," he sighed. "I saw a little raccoon eating out of our garbage can last night and it made me miss my raccoon-kitten."

"Oh, Ferdinand," said Lila. "Poor Soupy."

"It *would* be hard not to be able to visit your kitten," said Puff Puff. Puff Puff had *always* wanted to be a father.

All the cats were quiet for a minute.

"Well," said Spider Man, the bravest cat of the group. "Maybe we could go visit him." He looked around to see what everyone thought of his idea. "In the forest preserve."

Puff Puff's eyes almost popped out of his head. "What?!" The thought of venturing any farther than Soupy's porch scared him dreadfully.

A smile slowly spread across Soupy's face at the thought of seeing his son again.

"But what if a *dog* gets us?!," asked Puff Puff, looking all around.

Soupy's smile vanished. He had been chased by a very big dog once and it was a terrifying experi-ence. That was actually how he had gotten lost. He had run so far and so long from the dog that he couldn't find his way home again.

"I *want* to go to the forest preserve and find Ferdinand. I'm bored," pouted Lola. "We need a adventure!"

"*I'm* not afraid of dogs!," declared Spider Man, pointing at his chest with his thumb, although he had never seen one before.

"I wanna go to the forest, too," said Lila. Life can be a little boring sometimes when one is a cat because they don't get to go to school, or out to lunch, or to the movies like humans do.

Puff Puff licked his lips and looked toward home. He lived right next door to Soupy, too, on the west side. The other cats noticed Puff Puff's discomfort.

"Don't worry, Puff Puff," said Lila. "We won't be going today. We have to make a plan first."

"And when we go to the forest, someone needs to stay here to…umm…" Soupy touched his chin with his paw.

Spider Man realized what Soupy was trying to do and quickly added, "To report on what's going on here." He gestured around the neighborhood.

Soupy pointed at Spider Man. "Right!"

Puff Puff sighed in relief that they didn't expect him to go with them to the forest.

Spider Man stretched and yawned. "Well, guys, it's time for my catnap, so I'll see you tomorrow."

So the cats all agreed to come up with a plan to find Ferdinand and meet again the next morning on Soupy's porch to discuss their ideas. The biggest challenge would be sneaking Soupy out of the house without Molly or her father seeing.

Chapter 2
Soupy's Escape

The next day, after the cats gathered on the porch, Soupy began, "I can't try to escape when my Molly opens the door 'cause she watches me too carefully. She's ascared that I'll get lost again." Molly had been utterly heartbroken while Soupy was lost.

Lila said, "Well, I was thinking that Soupy could crouch under a table by the front door and wait for evil Billy to go outside, and then run outside when he opens the door." Evil Billy was Molly's big brother who enjoyed teasing her.

"Or maybe when Mr. Taylor leaves in the morning for work, Soupy could run out the door 'cause he's usually concentrating on holding his briefcase and his coffee," suggested Spider Man.

"That's true," nodded Lila. The cats had all seen Molly's father leave for work in the morning and it was quite a balancing act.

"Do you remember how to get back to the forest?," asked Spider Man, looking at Soupy.

All the cats looked at Soupy now.

"Oh sure," he said confidently. He pointed north. "It's that way about three blocks, across the field the whole way." Most cats have a great sense of direction…except when they're being chased by a huge cat-eating dog.

Puff Puff's eyes opened wide in fear. "*Three blocks*?! What if a dog gets you?!"

Everyone was silent for a moment. This was a good question.

"Well, since there'll be four of us, we can all watch in different directions, so a dog can't sneak up on us," said Lila. She bared her teeth and hissed softly at the thought of a dog sneaking up on them.

"Good idea," said Lola, nodding at Lila.

Puff Puff didn't feel assured that his friends would be safe from a dog attack but he highly doubted that he would be able to change their minds about trying to find Soupy's son. He looked toward the forest and shuddered.

"We'll be okay, Puff Puff," said Lola cheerily.

"I promise we'll come home safe," said Soupy.

Puff Puff swallowed and nodded.

❇ ❇ ❇

The next morning, Mr. Taylor got Molly and Billy off to camp and then hurried to the kitchen to get his briefcase and his coffee cup from the kitchen counter. Soupy got into position by the door under the coffee table. He crouched low and stayed perfectly still. When Mr. Taylor opened the door and stepped onto the porch, Soupy darted out the door, dashed to the edge of the porch, jumped the five feet down to the ground, and hid in a flower patch. Molly's father had no idea that his little girl's beloved cat had just run out of the house.

The other cats waited until Mr. Taylor drove off and then gathered back on the porch.

"Good job, Soupy!," said Lila, patting him on the back.

"I knew you could do it, Soup!," said Spider Man, smiling.

Puff Puff trembled.

Soupy looked around. It had been a year since he had been outside. He inhaled the fresh air and enjoyed the warm breeze.

"Now, be watchful, Puff Puff, while we're gone," said Lila, trying to make him feel useful.

Puff Puff stood on his hind legs and saluted Lila. "I will!"

Lila returned his salute. "As you were." They had learned this from Molly's Uncle Hal who was in the army.

Soupy said, "I'll lead 'cause I know the way there. So I'll watch for dogs up ahead."

"I'll be last, so I'll look out for dogs trying to sneak up on us from behind," said Spider Man.

Lila looked at Lola. "And Lila can look to her left and I'll look to my right."

Puff Puff bit his lower lip.

"We can run faster than dogs, Puff Puff," assured Soupy, although when he looked at how "husky" Spider Man was, he wasn't quite so sure about this.

Puff Puff tried to smile at Soupy.

Soupy, Lila, Lola, and Spider Man got into position.

"Ready?," asked Soupy, looking around at everyone.

"Yep," the other three cats answered in unison.

The little herd of cats walked toward the edge of the porch. But Puff Puff abruptly stood up.

"Wait!"

Soupy quickly came to a halt, causing Spider Man to bump into little Lola, which catapulted her off the porch!

"AAAAHHH!," she screamed as she flew through the air and then landed on the ground below with a thump.

Everyone ran to the edge of the porch and looked down but they didn't see Lola *anywhere*.

"LOLA!," screamed Lila.

"I'm okay!," called Lola but they still couldn't see her.

There was a tall patch of wildflowers a few feet away from the porch that began to wiggle and shake. A second later, Lola crawled out from among the flowers. "Whoa!," she said as she brushed herself off.

"I'm sorry, Lola!," said Spider Man, looking down at her and holding the side of his head with one paw.

"Don't worry. It was fun!," said Lola, giggling.

Spider Man smiled in relief and Lola quickly jumped back up on the porch.

She stood on the edge of the porch and looked down at the flower patch. "Do it again! Do it again, Spider Man!"

"Okay!," said Spider Man as he got into position and prepared to knock Lola into the flower patch again.

"No, no!" Lila wagged her paw at Spider Man and Lola. "Not now! Later, when we get back."

Lola and Spider Man's smiles disappeared. Lola glared at her sister and stomped the porch with her foot. "Bossy Bertha!," Lola mumbled under her breath.

"Puff Puff, why did you say 'wait?,'" asked Soupy, tilting his head at him.

"Wh'…when will you be back?," Puff Puff asked, looking toward the forest.

Everyone looked at Soupy.

"How long will we be gone," said Soupy thoughtfully. "We'll be back about the same time that my Molly gets home from camp."

Puff Puff raised his eyebrows. "*That* long?!" Molly and Billy came back from camp every day around 3:00 p.m.

"Well, we wanna give the forest a good search while we're there," explained Lila.

"Oh! And then if we do find my Ferdinand, we'll wanna visit with him for a while," said Soupy, blissfully imagining being reunited with his son.

Puff Puff just stared at them with his mouth hanging open.

"Stop worrying!," said Lila, becoming a little frustrated at her tiny worrywart friend.

Puff Puff became embarrassed. "Okay, go. G'… good luck." He tried to be brave and smile at his friends, but the expression on his face looked more like he had just bitten into a lemon.

"See you soon, Puff Puff," said little Lola.

Puff Puff just stood there with his lemon-biting expression on his tiny white face, too nervous to answer.

Soupy and his friends began walking toward the forest again. They jumped down from the porch one at a time. The group jogged the three blocks to the forest at a slow pace, careful not to tire out Spider Man. Whenever Soupy heard Spider Man breathing hard, he stopped for a rest.

After a few minutes, Soupy said, "We're almost there now." His nostrils flared and his eyes widened as he stared trancelike toward the forest…and his Ferdinand.

Chapter 3
Kitten

She was an only child and lived in the forest preserve with her mother. She called herself "Kitten" because that was what her mother had called her. A year ago, when Kitten was still small, her mother went off in search of food and had been struck by a car that was speeding down the street. After that, Kitten was left all alone in the world to fend for herself. She didn't know what happened to her mother; all she knew was that she walked off one day and never came back.

Kitten was extremely lonely after that and missed her mother very much. Out of her unbearable loneliness, she finally invented three imaginary friends for herself. They were sisters and their names were Shmoopy, Bopey, and Mopey. Shmoopy had curly blue fur and pointy tufts of fur on each ear. Bopey had long purple fur and a long mane. Mopey had short green-striped fur, a big ball of fur at the end of her tail, and being a direct descendant of a saber-toothed tiger, she had very long, sharp incisor teeth.

Sometimes Kitten, Shmoopy, and Bopey would ask Mopey why she had such big fangs. Mopey wasn't sure, so she would shrug her shoulders and simply say, "I don't know. Maybe *some* day they'll come in handy."

A few weeks ago, Kitten had given birth to two babies of her own, so she decided to change her name to "Momma." She had a boy kitten that she named Hoppy, who was orange and white, and she had a girl kitten that she named Squeaky who was a calico. Shortly after Momma met Boomerang, the father of her kittens, he moved away with his owner to another state.

Momma was utterly starving because she hadn't eaten in two days except for two little moths and a beetle that had tasted awful. Her babies had just fallen asleep, so she took the opportunity to search for something to eat. She wanted to visit Princess's house because Princess shared her food with her like she did with Soupy last summer when he was lost. But Momma was very tired of Princess's constant taunts. Princess could be very rude and usually made fun of Momma's ragged appearance. But Momma's hunger got the best of her. She sighed heavily and headed toward Princess's house. She stopped suddenly because she heard someone coming!

Oh no! A dog?!

She quickly crouched down in the tall grass. She peeked through the grass to see who it was. First, she saw an orange-striped boy, then a very big brown-striped boy, and then two black girls. The group was almost upon her now. Momma didn't know what to do, run or stay perfectly still and hope they passed without noticing her. Since she was weak with hunger, she decided to stay still and hope they didn't see her. But they were walking right toward her! And getting very close! Her breath quickened and she began to tremble.

"Oh!," Soupy exclaimed. He almost stepped on the skinny cat crouching low in the grass. "Hi! I didn't see you there." The cat looked very scared. "Are you okay?" Soupy lifted his eyebrows at the poor cat.

Spider Man, Lila, and Lola scurried closer to Soupy, curious to see who he was talking to. Momma looked up at the group with wide eyes, too afraid to speak. But they looked friendly.

"H'…hi," she said, blinking quickly several times.

"Who are you hiding from?," whispered the small black girl. "A dog?" Lola looked all around for an approaching dog.

"Oh…no, not a dog," Momma bit her lip nervously. "I guess I'm hiding from *you*."

"Oh! You don't have to hide from us, Miss. We won't hurt you," said the big boy.

"My name is Lila," the silky, tall black girl said. She gestured toward the smaller black girl. "And this is Lola, my little sister, and this is Spider Man." She gestured toward the chubby boy. "And this is Soupy." She touched the handsome orange-striped boy's shoulder.

"Hi," replied Momma as she stood up.

The cats waited for Momma to introduce herself, but after a few seconds of silence, Lola asked, "And what's *your* name?"

Momma cleared her throat. "Oh. My name is...um...'Momma.'"

The group was silent for a moment.

Lola asked, "Momma?" She tilted her head at Momma.

Momma nodded. She wondered what was wrong with her name.

Soupy thought about how his Molly called her mother "Mom" but her father called her "Michelle."

"But what is your...other name?," asked Soupy.

Momma thought for a second. "No." She shook her head. "I'm only 'Momma.'"

"But what did your owner name you?," Lila asked.

"Owner?," asked Momma. "What's a 'owner?'"

"Well, me and Lola live with Cindy and Steve and they gave us our names. And Soupy's Molly named him Soupy 'cause he drank her soup when he was a kitten. And Spider Man's owner, Marcy, let her grandkittens, Ruby and Frankie, name him. What did *your* owner name *you*?"

"Oh,..." Momma shook her head. "I don't have a owner."

The cats looked at Momma blankly.

"Well where do you live then?!," Lola blurted out.

Momma looked at Lola. "Here, in the forest." She gestured toward the forest.

The cats all looked at Momma again for a long moment. About two inches of her tail and the tips of her ears had frozen off in the bitter cold winter. Her left incisor tooth was chipped because she had run in a panic into a large rock while being chased by a dog one day. One of her front paws stuck straight out from her ankle because she had been hit by a car and had never received medical treatment to set the bone straight again. All that remained of her left eye was a sunken hole because she had contracted an upper respiratory virus that had also gone untreated. The insides of Momma's ears were dirty and bloody because she had ear mites, and the cats could see every one of her ribs. She was even thinner than Soupy had been when he had come home from the forest.

Momma noticed the cats looking her over and worried that they were going to make fun of her like Princess always did. Princess taunted her with cruel names, such as "Snaggle-Tooth" and "The One-Eyed Monster." Momma's stomach growled and she looked toward Princess's house.

If I'm gonna be teased by someone, I choose Princess 'cause at least I'll get a little food in my belly, thought Momma.

"Well," said Lila cheerily. "Well, *we* could give you a name."

Momma looked at Lila, surprised that she wasn't making fun of her. "You...you could?"

"Sure!," said Lila. "It'll be fun!"

"Oh," Momma smiled. "That would be nice." Momma licked her paw a few times and then rubbed her face with it to look her best.

"Okay, guys, what do you think we should name Momma?," Lila asked.

Momma feverishly scratched her side where a flea was biting her.

"Hmmm," said Spider Man. "I've never named anyone before."

Soupy looked at poor Momma and said, "How 'bout 'Bella?' It means 'pretty' I think."

Momma quickly turned toward Soupy and looked at him suspiciously. She *knew* she wasn't pretty. Princess had made sure of that. But Soupy was smiling at her kindly.

"That's a pretty name," said Lola. Lola suddenly chased after a little moth that flew by.

Spider Man looked at Momma's sunken-in eye socket and her chipped tooth and said, "How about

'Beau?' I think that means 'pretty' in French." His Marcy was taking French lessons.

Momma whirled her head around to look at Spider Man. Now she was *sure* they were making fun of her. But Spider Man had a kind smile on his face, too. A bumblebee buzzed by then and Spider Man dashed after it.

"Why don't we let Momma choose," said Lila. "Momma, do you like either of those names, 'Beau' or 'Bella?'"

The bumble bee eluded Spider Man, so he returned to the group. All the cats looked at Momma now for her decision. She grimaced and scratched her ear with her hind leg where an ear mite was biting her.

"They're both nice," said Momma when she was done scratching. She thought for a moment about which name she liked better. She felt very important right then with all the cats looking at her, waiting for her decision.

"I think I choose…," Momma put a paw to her chin and looked up at the sky, trying to draw out the attention she was receiving. "'Beau!,'" she said, nodding once.

"Ah, good choice," said Spider Man. "Beau" had been *his* suggestion.

"Yes, it suits you, Momma," said Lola. "Oh! I mean *Beau*!," she laughed.

Soupy crossed his arms in front of his chest and pouted because Momma hadn't chosen his suggestion of "Bella."

"So, *Beau*, why did you call yourself 'Momma?' Do you have kittens?," asked Lila, wide-eyed.

"Yes," answered Beau. "I have two kittens."

Lola gasped. "You do?!"

"Yup."

"Can we see 'em?!," Soupy asked, shifting from paw to paw.

Beau looked in the direction of Princess's house again. She was unbearably hungry but didn't want to be rude to these sweet cats who gave her a name and didn't make fun of her.

"Sure! Follow me," said Beau. She walked back toward the forest preserve, and Spider Man, Soupy, Lola, and Lila walked close behind her smiling in anticipation.

"We love kittens!," explained Spider Man to Beau.

Right at the edge of the forest, deep inside some tall grass, Beau stopped. She walked into the tall grass and looked down. The other cats walked carefully behind her and looked down, too. There, snuggled close together, were her two tiny babies, fast asleep.

"Oh my gosh!," whispered Lola in wonder, covering her mouth with one paw.

"They're so cute!," said Lila quietly.

Beau beamed with pride.

"Kittens…," said Soupy dreamily, remembering when his Ferdinand was tiny.

"I wish *I* had a kitten," said Spider Man wistfully.

Even though the cats had spoken very quietly, the tiny calico kitten stirred and stretched. She smelled her mother and quickly opened her eyes and looked around for her. When she saw Beau, she squeaked loudly three times and scrambled to her feet. Beau laid down next to her babies, circling them with her body. The kitten crawled over her brother to get to Beau, waking him, too. The other kitten stood up and took two little hops over to Beau, and they both started nursing.

"They're so small!," said Lila.

Beau looked lovingly at her babies.

"What are their names?," asked Spider Man.

"Well, this is Squeaky." She touched the little calico kitten on the head. "And this one," Beau licked the orange and white kitten on the head, "is Hoppy."

Beau's stomach growled. Embarrassed, she cleared her throat and looked around as if to see where the noise had come from.

"Ooh, you must be hungry," said Soupy, remembering how difficult it was to find food in the forest preserve.

"I'm starving!," said Beau. "I was on my way to Princess's house to see if she would let me eat from her bowl when you all came along."

Soupy's eyes widened. "Princess?! You know Princess?"

"Yes!," said Beau, looking curiously at Soupy. "You do, too?"

Soupy frowned and nodded slowly, remembering how rude Princess could be. Beau squinted her eye and nodded back at Soupy in understanding.

"When I was lost last summer, Princess used to let me eat from her bowl, too. But sometimes, she can be...," Soupy hesitated because he didn't like to say bad things about anyone.

"She can be very *rude*!," Lila finished Soupy's sentence for him. Lila didn't like rude cats and had always wanted to meet Princess so that she could hiss at her and tell her off.

Soupy grinned. Beau was glad to hear that Princess's rudeness wasn't all reserved just for her.

"She makes fun of me all the time," said Beau, pouting.

Lila growled and bared her teeth at the thought of Princess. Beau seemed very sweet and there was no excuse for Princess's cruelty. "Just wait'll I meet this…this '*Princess.*'" Lila's face skewed up when she said "Princess" as if she were talking about something that one would find in a litter box.

Little Lola's nails extended involuntarily at the thought of this Princess cat, first being mean to Soupy and now to Beau. Lola wanted to scratch Princess' eyes out right then and there. But she didn't say anything because Lila had taught her that cats are not allowed to scratch anyone's eyes out no matter how much they deserved it.

*But I still **want** to!* thought Lola, baring her teeth and spitting softly two times.

"Well," said Spider Man, "We have to get you some food!" A lightening bug flew by and he ran after it.

"Right!," said Lola, watching her chubby friend try to catch the bug, which flew just out of his reach.

"Let's run home and try to find something for Beau to eat," said Soupy, remembering how hungry he always was when he lived in the forest.

Lila thought about having to wait for Spider Man to catch his breath whenever they ran. "Why don't you stay here and keep Beau company, Spider Man."

"Sure!," said Spider Man quickly, grateful that he didn't have to make the trip again.

They're going to feed me?! "Well,…thank you so much," Beau said shyly.

"You're welcome!," said Lila.

"Let's go," said Soupy.

And off they sped toward home. They were home again within minutes.

Chapter 4
Finding Food for Beau

Puff Puff heard his friends returning and smiled. He stood up excitedly to greet them.

"You're back!," he said happily but he saw that Spider Man wasn't with them and his jaw dropped.

"Where's Spider Man?!" Puff Puff placed a paw over his heart. "Did a dog eat 'im?!" He felt faint and stumbled backwards.

"No! He's fine, Puff Puff! He just stayed with Beau," answered Soupy quickly.

"We're only home to try to find some food for this momma cat that we met by the forest," added Lila.

"She's starving!," said Lola.

"You met a new cat?! By the forest?!"

"Yes! And she has *kittens*!," said Lola excitedly.

"Kittens?!" Puff Puff's eyes widened.

"Okay, let's all go home and see what kind of food we can find for Beau," said Lila.

And with that, Puff Puff, Lila, and Lola ran home.

Lila and Lola ran through their cat door into the kitchen and jumped right up on the counter where Cindy always defrosted that night's dinner. The girls were both happy to see two steaks sitting there. They turned to each other and smiled. They knew they weren't supposed to help themselves to Cindy and Steve's food but Beau was starving. They both stood very still and listened for the where-abouts of their owners. Everything was perfectly quiet, so they determined they weren't home.

"Well, I think…," said Lila, looking up at the ceiling thoughtfully. "That they would *want* us to give one of their steaks to Beau instead of keeping it for themselves, don't you?"

"Well," thought Lola, holding her paw to her chin. "I'm sure if they knew how hungry Beau is, they would be *more* than happy to give her their steak." She gestured toward the steaks.

The truth was that Lila and Lola were com-pletely correct in their thinking. Cindy and Steve loved animals very much and if they knew that there was a cat starving in the forest, they would gladly give her their steak.

At that, Lila scratched away the plastic wrap from the steaks, grabbed the bigger steak in her mouth, and jumped off the counter.

The girls ran back to Soupy's porch and waited for Puff Puff.

Puff Puff's 8-year-old owner, Carli Adler, was sitting at the kitchen table, trying to finish the big ham steak her mother had cooked for her for breakfast. Carli usually loved ham steak for break- fast but she had woken up early that morning and had snuck into the kitchen cabinet and stole seven cookies. She munched on the cookies while she watched her favorite cartoons and wasn't hungry now for breakfast. Carli had only taken two small bites out of the ham so far and was plotting how she was going to get rid of the rest without eating it. Snacking before meals was strictly forbidden in the Adler household, so Carli couldn't admit to her mother why she wasn't hungry this morning.

Where's Puff Puff? Carli looked around the kitchen for him. *He'd be happy to help me eat this **poopy** ham!*

She glared at the back of her mother' head for giving her so much food. Just then, Puff Puff came running through his cat door and Carli grinned. She looked up at her mother to see if she was watching but she was busy washing the dishes. Carli quickly held out the ham to Puff Puff under the table. He snatched it in his mouth and immediately dashed out his cat door. Carli quickly looked at her mother to see if she had seen Puff Puff running away with the ham, but she was still facing the sink.

"I'm done!," said Carli jubilantly, bouncing in her chair.

Mrs. Adler turned around to see if she had cleaned her plate properly.

"Oh, well. It's about time!," she said. "You're excused. Go play."

"Yaaay!," said Carli as she ran outside to play.

Puff Puff ran back to the porch and found Lila and Lola there with a big steak at their feet. Puff Puff placed his ham at his feet, too.

"I'll carry Puff Puff's ham to Beau. Okay, are we ready to go then?," asked Soupy very business-like, remembering what it was like to be starving.

"Sure," said Lila.

"See you later, Puff Puff," said Lola.

"Wait!," said Puff Puff, biting his nail.

Lila, Lola, and Soupy stopped and looked at Puff Puff but he said nothing. He looked in the direction of the forest.

"Um...do you want to go with us, Puff Puff?," asked Soupy.

Puff Puff bit his lip. He adored kittens. But he was very scared to leave the porch...for *anything*.

Soupy, Lila, and Lola could see Puff Puff struggling with his decision.

"We'll be with you the whole time," assured Soupy, nodding encouragingly.

"We already got there and back safely once," said Lila.

Puff Puff blinked several times, thinking.

"You could just *try* going with us," said Lola slowly. "If you change your mind, you can turn back."

Puff Puff wanted to see the kittens with all his heart. He took a deep breath. "I'm coming with you!"

"Okay!," said Soupy, proud of his tiny, timid friend.

Lila picked up the steak and Puff Puff picked up his ham and they walked to the end of the porch and jumped off. They were careful to keep Puff Puff in the middle of the pack to help him feel safe. They could see the fear in his eyes as they ran toward the forest. The steak was heavy, so Lila, Lola, and Soupy took turns carrying it.

They ran across the large field and saw Spider Man standing near the edge of the forest.

"Hi," Spider Man called from across the field. He saw Puff Puff coming, too, and couldn't believe his eyes. "Puff Puff?!" He blinked twice and looked again to make sure he wasn't imagining it.

Puff Puff couldn't answer Spider Man because he had the ham in his mouth but he darted now as fast as his little legs would carry him toward Spider Man. Lila, Lola, and Soupy couldn't keep up with him.

"What is a 'Puff Puff?,'" asked Beau, still lying next to her babies in the grass, although they had finished nursing and were wrestling with each other now.

Spider Man looked down at Beau. "Oh, that's another friend of ours. He's a little scaredy-cat, so he didn't want to come with us earlier. But he's coming now! I can't believe it!," explained Spider Man. He quickly added, "Oh, don't tell him I called him a scaredy-cat! He likes to think of himself as macho."

Beau covered her mouth with her paw and giggled. "Oh, I won't, don't worry." She knew how hurtful it was to be insulted, so she wouldn't *think* of doing it to someone else. She stood up to see Puff Puff. "Boy, he *is* tiny!"

"Yes, he's tiny, but he has a *very* big heart," said Spider Man.

"Ah." Beau smiled. "What's in his mouth?"

Puff Puff was getting closer, so Spider Man could see what it was now. "Oh, it's ham. You'll like that."

Food?! Beau's eyes widened. She looked toward the approaching tiny Puff Puff kitty.

When Puff Puff arrived, he plunked the large piece of ham on the ground right in front of Beau. The smell was irresistible but she controlled herself until she was properly introduced. Puff Puff looked at Beau and Beau became nervous again that he might make a rude comment about her looks, but he just smiled widely at her, so happy to meet her.

"Puff Puff, this is Beau. Beau, this is Puff Puff," said Spider Man.

"Hi, Beau!" Puff Puff couldn't stop smiling.

"Hi. Thank you so much for bringing me this ham. I'm starving!"

"Eat!," said tiny Puff Puff. He motioned toward the ham.

That was all Beau needed. She took a huge bite of the ham and chewed it only twice and swallowed. She had never tasted anything so good in her life. She finished the ham in twenty seconds.

Meanwhile, Lila, Lola, and Soupy reached the group now, too. Lila plopped the big steak at Beau's feet.

Beau inhaled deeply and her mouth watered. "What's this?!" The smell was divine.

"This is what you call a steak," said Lila. "Eat up."

That was enough for Beau. She immediately started eating the steak. It was so delicious that Beau went into a trance, thinking of nothing else until only the bone was left.

While Beau ate, Puff Puff looked around at his surroundings. The long field he had just run across and the edge of the forest. He couldn't even see their houses. He couldn't believe that he had traveled so far away from the safety of Soupy's porch.

Puff Puff felt very brave. He peered into the thick green forest and wondered what it was like. He thought maybe someday, he might even be brave enough to enter the forest and go exploring, maybe with Soupy and Ferdinand.

Beau's belly was full now, a sensation she was not used to.

"I've never tasted anything so good in my life! Thank you so much," she said looking around at the cats. Beau promptly started licking her paw and washing her face and ears.

"Welcome!," said Lila.

Beau's heart overflowed with emotion. The first time she met Princess, Princess told her that she couldn't come into her house to eat because she didn't want her dirtying up her kitchen.

Beau noticed Puff Puff staring at the kittens in awe.

"These are my kittens, Puff Puff. This is Squeaky," she said as she touched tiny Squeaky on her head. Squeaky looked up at her mother and squeaked at her. "And this is Hoppy."

"They're so tiny," said Puff Puff. "I *love* them!," he blurted out. Then he became embarrassed. But Beau just smiled proudly at him.

The other cats laughed, though, and Puff Puff frowned.

Soupy said, "It's okay, Puff Puff, *everybody* loves kittens!"

Puff Puff laughed, too, then. Beau yawned.

"Why don't you take a catnap, Beau, and I'll kitten-sit for you," offered Puff Puff.

"Really? I am really sleepy all of a sudden," said Beau.

"Sure!," said Puff Puff.

Beau looked around again into her new friends' kind faces. She smiled and laid down in the grass next to her kittens. She put her paw over her eyes and quickly fell asleep. The kittens were sleeping again, too, and since it was time for a catnap for the rest of the cats, everyone laid down and took a nice nap in the warm sun together.

Chapter 5
Looking for Ferdinand

About two hours later, Puff Puff woke up slowly. He stretched and yawned. He opened his eyes slowly and saw that he was nose to nose with the kitten named Squeaky.

"Oh!," said Puff Puff.

"Daddah?," asked Squeaky in a squeaky little voice.

Puff Puff smiled. "Hi, Squeaky."

Squeaky smelled Puff Puff's nose. It tickled so Puff Puff's nose twitched a little. Then she smelled his eye for a moment. Puff Puff closed his eyes while she did this. Then she backed away from him. Puff Puff opened his eyes and looked into her adorable face.

"How are you today, Squeaky?," he asked. Squeaky's cute little face skewed up into a sneer. She scurried up to him and answered him with two quick swats to the side of his face.

"Oh!," laughed Puff Puff. "You're *very* tough."

Squeaky crouched down on the ground look-ing intently at Puff Puff. She shifted her weight from one back foot to the other, securing her footing in the ground. This caused her tiny bottom to wiggle back and forth. Puff Puff knew what was coming and braced himself. Squeaky pounced on Puff Puff's head and bit his ear and Puff Puff laughed. Squeaky pulled right and left on his ear with all her might.

"Cut that out, silly."

Squeaky grabbed Puff Puff's neck from behind with both arms and bit him as hard as she could. Her teeth were so tiny though that they didn't go all the way through his fluffy fur to his skin.

Hoppy woke up, too, and he hopped over to each cat and smelled them carefully. Hoppy sniffed Lila's face and Lila licked his tiny head. He liked this so he leaned against Lila and purred. Lila continued washing him.

Beau woke up and saw her babies playing with her new friends. She smiled. It was so nice to have company.

Soupy suddenly remembered why they had made the trip to forest in the first place.

"I'm gonna go look for Ferdinand."

All the cats looked up from the kittens. In the excitement of meeting a new cat and her kittens, they had forgotten about their original reason for coming to the forest.

"Oh, poor Soupy! We forgot about Ferdinand!," said little Lola, looking at him apologetically.

"Who's Ferdinand?," asked Beau, looking at Soupy.

"He's my foster son. I found him in the forest last summer when I was lost. He was a tiny baby and I raised him."

"Why didn't you bring him with you when you found your way home?," asked Beau.

"'Cause he was a *raccoon*-kitten," said Soupy, nodding and closing his eyes.

"Oh!," said Beau. She was familiar with raccoons. "So your 'kitten' grew up to be twice as big as you!," she laughed.

Soupy smiled at Beau. "Yep, he was a very big boy!," he said wistfully. He looked toward the forest.

"Go, Soupy. Go find Ferdinand. Do you want me to go with you?," offered Lila.

"No thanks. I can move faster alone."

"Okay, good luck!," said Lila.

"Good luck!," said the others together.

Soupy smiled, turned, and quickly ran into the forest. It looked much the same as it had the year before. He ran down to the creek calling "FERDI-NAAAAAAAND!" There was no response. He drank from the creek for a moment. He ran north for a while and screamed "FERDINAAAAND!" He waited and listened but no one answered.

"FEEEEEERDINAAAAAAND!," he tried again. Soupy looked all around the forest. Nothing stirred.

Where can he be?

He ran back to the other cats, worried that it was getting late. It was around 3:00 p.m. now. When he arrived at the edge of the forest where the cats and kittens were playing together, they heard him coming from the crunching of the twigs under his paws.

"Did you find him?," asked Spider Man.

All the cats quickly stood up and peered behind Soupy to see if a raccoon was following him.

He shook his head. "No."

Everyone's face fell.

Lila patted Soupy's back.

"You'll find him tomorrow," said little Lola, nodding.

Spider Man looked at Beau. "We better get going now, Beau."

"Oh?," she said sadly, looking around at all the cats.

Puff Puff noticed her sadness and said, "But we'll be back tomorrow. I promise!"

Beau smiled broadly. "Really?!"

"Well, I'll be back," said Puff Puff, looking at the other cats.

"I'm coming back tomorrow, too," said Soupy. He wanted to search for Ferdinand again and bring poor Beau more food.

"Me, too," said Spider Man. "And we'll bring more food."

Beau's eyes widened and she licked her lips. "You're all so…kind…" Her voice broke off.

Puff Puff kissed the kittens good bye. He hated to leave them.

"Good bye, babies," said Lola, nuzzling each kitten.

Without having to carry the ham or the steak, the cats were home again in four minutes. It would have only taken three if they hadn't needed to stop a couple of times for Spider Man to catch his breath.

When they arrived home, the bus was in front of Soupy's house, returning Billy and Molly from summer camp. The cats saw Billy get off the bus first.

"Quick, Soupy! Get into position on the porch!," urged Spider Man.

"Hurry!," exclaimed Lola.

Soupy jumped up on the porch and hid under the porch bench. Billy ran to the front door, not noticing Soupy, unlocked the door, and hurried inside. He left the door open for Molly, so Soupy dashed inside right behind him. Molly was concentrating on holding the railing tightly and climbing down the tall steps of the bus with her backpack, so she didn't see Soupy run inside the house after Billy. She had fallen down the bus stairs once and scraped her hands and knees, so she was extra careful now. Soupy ran to the TV room, jumped onto the couch, and laid down, pretending like he had been there all day just waiting for his Molly to return. Molly immediately ran to the TV room to find Soupy.

"There's my Soupy!," she said.

Molly had a rough day at camp. At lunch when she took a bite of her sandwich, a big glob of jelly had squeezed out and plopped onto her white shirt. When she tried to wipe it with her napkin, she just smeared it around into a much bigger purple splotch. For the rest of the day, whenever the camp counselors weren't close enough to hear, the other children called her "The Creature from the Purple Lagoon."

"You're the most handsomest cat in the whole wide world!," Molly told Soupy, and he beamed. Molly quickly climbed up on the couch, picked up Soupy, and buried her face into the back of his neck, taking comfort from her soft, warm cat who loved her no matter how messy she was.

"I love you so much!," said Molly. Soupy purred. He was horribly disappointed that he hadn't been able to find his *raccoon*-kitten that day but he felt better now that he was with his *human*-kitten again. Molly held Soupy for several minutes and then placed him on the couch beside her. She turned the TV on and found a show that she liked. Soupy put his elbow on Molly's lap and his head down on his arm and quickly fell asleep while she petted him softly. He dreamed of Ferdinand again.

As soon as the other cats saw Soupy get into his house, they said goodbye and went home, too.

❋ ❋ ❋

After her new friends left, Beau heard leaves crackling near the forest's edge. She quickly turned and saw something purple and something blue through the forest trees approaching. It was Shmoopy and Bopey coming to visit.

"Hi Shmoopy! Hi, Bopey! Where's Mopey?"

"She's coming," answered Shmoopy and Bopey together. They looked back into the forest where Mopey was straggling slowly behind them yawning.

"I'm comin'. I'm comin'," said Mopey lazily.

When Mopey caught up to her sisters, Beau excitedly told them all about her new friends and how they had brought her food to eat. Shmoopy, Bopey, and Mopey seemed a little jealous at first but they were happy that Beau had some food in her belly.

Chapter 6
The Big Ugly Monsters

Beau woke up the next morning in the forest with her kittens sleeping next to her. She wondered if her new wonderful friends would keep their promise and visit her again today…and with more food for her to eat. Her new friends seemed too good to be true. They gave her a very nice name, they didn't make fun of her appearance, and they brought her *food*. Beau didn't even know that such delicious food *existed* in the world. She was beginning to worry that it might all have been just a wonderful dream.

❊ ❊ ❊

The next day, Soupy waited by the front door for Molly's father to leave for work and he successfully escaped again without being noticed. After Mr. Taylor drove off, Soupy jumped back up on the porch and waited for Lola, Lila, Puff Puff, and Spider Man. Ten minutes later, everyone had gathered on the porch. Puff Puff brought a fried egg in his mouth and Lola had a hamburger patty that Cindy had reheated for breakfast but then left on her plate. Spider Man had meowed at Marcy and pawed at her leg during breakfast, so she had given him a big piece of bacon. Molly and Billy had only eaten cereal for breakfast, so Soupy wasn't able to pilfer anything for Beau. So he was very happy to see that his friends had all been able to find food for her.

"Are we ready to go?," asked Puff Puff, anxious to see the kittens again.

"Yep. Let's go!," said Spider Man.

The cats picked up their food and off they went to the forest. Beau was sitting up watching for them but Spider Man saw her first.

"Hi, Beau!," he called. It came out very muffled because of the bacon in his mouth.

Beau's face lit up. *They kept their promise!* She shifted from paw to paw excitedly.

"Hi!," she said, trembling with happiness. Her kittens clamored around her feet, watching the approaching group of cats.

The group picked up their pace now and joined Beau and her kittens quickly. They dropped the fried egg, bacon, and hamburger at her feet. The food smelled wonderful. Beau inhaled deeply and her mouth watered.

"Oh thank you!," said Beau.

"Eat up!," said Lila cheerily.

Beau ate the hamburger first.

"That was so good! What was that?," she asked.

"That was a hamburger," said Lola.

Beau ate the bacon next and then gobbled up the egg in just four bites.

"What was that...other stuff," asked Beau.

"Oh, what I brought is called bacon," explained Spider Man.

"What I brought is called a egg," said Puff Puff.

"Mmmm. Very yummy! Thank you very much for bringing me bacon, and a egg, and a h'...hangaburger," said Beau. She scratched feverishly at a flea that was biting her shoulder.

A grasshopper hopped by and Lila tried to pounce on it. Puff Puff lied down next to tiny Squeaky.

"Daddah!," squeaked Squeaky. She smacked Puff Puff on the side of his face two times and Puff Puff chuckled. He barely felt the smacks through his long fur. Then she immediately jumped on Puff Puff's back and bit the top of his head. Puff Puff wiggled his head so that Squeaky wiggled back and forth, too.

As soon as tiny Hoppy saw Spider Man, he hopped over to him, grabbed his front leg, and bit it. Spider Man smiled and washed the top of Hoppy's head.

Beau belched loudly! "OH!" She covered her mouth with both paws. "Excuse me!"

The other cats just laughed, so she laughed too.

"So what are these 'owners' that you talked about?," asked Beau. She winced and scratched the inside of her ear.

"Well, do you wanna see them?," asked Lila. Cindy and Steve were gardening in the backyard.

"Sure!," said Beau.

"Okay, come on," said Lila. "Can you guys stay here and watch Beau's kittens?"

"Sure!," said the rest of the cats.

Lila and Beau jogged across the large field and a few minutes later, they were close enough to Lila's house to see Cindy and Steve in the back yard. Beau abruptly stopped in her tracks.

"What's wrong," asked Lila.

"I'm not going over by those…those big, ugly monsters," said Beau.

"Big ugly monsters?," Lila quickly looked around but didn't see any big ugly monsters anywhere.

"Right there," said Beau, pointing at Cindy and Steve. Lila looked where Beau was pointing and was fairly sure that she was pointing right at her beloved Cindy and Steve! She looked back at Beau with her mouth open.

"Those ugly monsters are mean!," said Beau, frowning.

Lila looked again at Cindy and Steve. She couldn't *believe* that Beau had just called them "ugly monsters." Lila thought that her Cindy and Steve were beautimous! Although she did think they would look even better if they had fur on their faces. But she thought *all* humans would be much better looking if they had fur.

Beau had some very bad experiences with humans in the past. A few months earlier, a teenage boy had shot her in the leg with a BB gun. The BB passed through the muscle of her leg, it didn't hit the bone, but it had terrified Beau and had been very painful. Another time when Beau was walking through a backyard, a big ugly monster had come running out of its house screaming like a boiling teakettle and carrying a broom. The monster chased Beau and tried to beat her with the broom. Beau had escaped by the tip of her short tail.

Beau could see that Lila didn't understand, so she explained, "One time, a monster chased me and tried to beat me with a big stick. Another time, a monster pointed a wooden thing at me and there was a boom and then something shot through my leg, and…and I limped for a long time," she stuttered.

"Oh!," said Lila. She covered her mouth with her paw and stared at Beau wide-eyed. Lila had never heard of humans acting so horrible. "That's awful." She patted Beau's shoulder and Beau smiled bravely at Lila.

Beau looked at Cindy and Steve warily and then looked back toward the forest. She just wanted to go back to her kittens.

"So…where are your 'owners?,'" asked Beau, looking at Lila.

"Um,…" Lila bit her lip. "Those 'monsters' over there…" She pointed at Cindy and Steve. "*Are* my 'owners.'"

Beau's face went slack. She stared at Lila in disbelief. "No! Those *ugly monsters* are your… 'OWNERS?'"

"Yes!" Lila nodded. "And they're called 'humans,' not 'monsters.'" Lila held her paw up to her mouth and giggled a little.

Beau was speechless.

"But they're really nice. They never point anything at us that shoots stuff, and they never chase us with big sticks or scream at us. I promise!"

Beau just blinked at Lila several times and looked toward the forest again wistfully.

"Do you want to come and meet them with me?," asked Lila hopefully.

"NO!" Beau quickly shook her head. "No, no, no, no!" She closed her eyes and shook her head back and forth over and over again.

Lila wasn't surprised. She sighed heavily.

"Well, how about you watch me go over to them, so you can see how nice they are to *me*?"

"No!" Beau didn't want to see her new friend get eaten by the ugly monsters.

"I've lived with them for my whole life, five winters."

Beau just sat there silently watching Cindy and Steve. She gulped.

"Stay here and watch." Lila touched Beau's shoulder.

Beau trembled as she watched Lila run toward the monsters.

"Hello, Miss Lila!," said Steve when he saw her coming. He took off his garden gloves and picked her up and snuggled her. Out in the field, Beau held her breath and watched in horror, expecting Steve to take a big bite out of Lila. Lila rubbed her face against Steve's cheek and purred.

Cindy stopped pruning the apple tree and walked over to Steve to pet Lila.

"Hello silky girl," said Cindy lovingly. Lila purred louder.

Off in the field, Beau could hear the monsters talking to Lila in soft, sweet tones. She watched as they petted her and kissed her.

"Where's your sister?," asked Cindy. Lila and Lola were rarely apart.

"Yeah, where *is* your little sister?," asked Steve. He looked around for Lola.

Cindy noticed a cat standing out in the field.

"Look, a cat." She pointed at Beau.

Steve turned to look where Cindy was pointing and saw Beau.

He squinted. "That's a skinny cat!"

Cindy squinted at Beau and said, "You're right. Poor thing. Do you think it's a stray?"

"Yeah, I bet it is."

"Hey!," said Cindy. "Maybe that's where one of our steaks went yesterday."

"You think the stray cat snuck into the house and stole our steak?," laughed Steve.

Cindy giggled. "Well maybe it smelled the steak and came through the cat door...or else Lila and Lola took it and brought it to her?" But as she said it, that sounded a little unlikely.

"We could give it a test. Let's give Lila something to eat, something she can carry, and see if she brings it to the stray," said Steve.

Cindy pointed at her husband. "Clever! I'll go get something."

Cindy hurried into the kitchen and opened the refrigerator. She saw some slices of ham and brought a piece out to Lila. Lila loved ham and always gobbled it up right away whenever they gave her some.

"Okay, put her down," instructed Cindy.

Steve placed Lila in the grass and Cindy held the ham out to her. Lila grabbed it in her mouth and immediately ran toward the skinny cat out in the field.

Cindy and Steve looked at each other in amazement. They watched as Lila plopped the ham at the cat's feet and saw her gobble it up in three bites, barely chewing it.

"Oh my gosh! I don't believe this!," exclaimed Cindy.

"Me neither," said Steve.

"Well, we have to catch that poor cat and…"

"I knew you'd say that," interrupted Steve. "Two cats is *enough*!"

"Oh, what's one more little cat? You won't even notice," said Cindy, frowning at her husband.

"Besides, it's probably feral," said Steve, trying to discourage Cindy from taking in a third cat.

"Well, we can try to tame it if it's feral. And if we can't tame it, we can at least trap it, take it to the vet for shots and medicine, and get it neutered or spayed," she gestured toward Beau. "So that there aren't more stray kittens born in the wild to starve like she obviously is," said Cindy righteously.

Steve sighed. "You're right. We need to help the cat. It's very rough living in the wild."

"That's right," said Cindy, smiling gratefully at her husband. "I'm gonna go see if the cat will let me pet her. You stay here."

Cindy started walking slowly toward Lila and the new kitty. Beau noticed Cindy approaching.

"What's the ugly monster...I mean what's your 'owner' doing?!," asked Beau. "She's coming our way!" Beau's eyes widened and she started backing up.

"Here kitty, kitty, kitty," said Cindy walking slowly toward Beau, holding out her hand toward her.

"She probably just wants to meet you..." Lila looked at Beau and saw her backing up toward the forest.

"No! Don't go!," Lila pleaded.

"Does she have a stick?!," asked Beau, beginning to panic. "Or something to shoot me with?!"

"No!," said Lila. "She would NEVER do that!" But Beau kept inching away from the approaching Cindy Monster.

"I'M GOING BACK!," yelled Beau. And she quickly ran toward the forest.

"WAIT, BEAU!," screamed Lila.

Beau stopped and looked back at Lila. She looked toward Cindy then and saw that she was now returning to her backyard. Beau sighed in relief.

"I'm sorry," said Beau. "I'll meet your Cindy Monster another day, k?" Beau wasn't sure about this but she felt that she should say *something* to Lila.

"It's okay. Don't feel bad," said Lila. "If humans shot me and chased me with a big stick, I'd be ascared, too."

Beau smiled gratefully at Lila.

"Let's go back."

❋ ❋ ❋

"Well, at least you tried," said Steve to Cindy when she was back in their yard again.

"Oh, no, no, no, no, noooo!," said Cindy, wagging her finger in her husband's face. "I'm not giving up *that* easily."

"Oh, I know that!," said Steve. His wife was *very* devoted to helping animals.

"That poor little cat looks like a walking skeleton!," said Cindy with great concern on her face.

"Well, I'm sure you'll fatten her up," said Steve putting his gardening gloves back on.

Cindy smiled, already mentally adding items to her grocery list that Lila and Lola could carry off to their new skeletal friend.

❈ ❈ ❈

When Lila and Beau reached the other cats and the kittens, Lila giggled and reported that, "Beau called Cindy and Steve 'ugly monsters!'"

"Ugly monsters!?," exclaimed little Lola, quickly turning toward Beau. "They are not! They're beautimous!"

"Oh, I was just kidding," said Beau quickly. She felt bad about accidentally insulting their owners when Lola and Lila had been so nice to her.

"There were some humans who were very mean to Beau," explained Lila. "One shot something through her leg and another tried to beat her with a stick!"

"No!," exclaimed Puff Puff. He stared at Beau with his mouth hanging open.

"That's horrible!," gasped Lola.

"No wonder you think they're *monsters*!," said Soupy.

"All our owners are very nice," said Spider Man, nodding quickly.

"Really?," said Beau, finding this difficult to believe.

"Really!," said Spider Man. "My Marcy holds me, and pets me, and gives me lots of yummy treats."

Beau looked at Spider Man's chubby body and thought *It sure **looks** like you get lots of treats!* but then she immediately felt bad for thinking it.

"And they don't try to eat you?," asked Beau, scratching her ear.

"No!," they all said in unison, laughing. Beau smiled sheepishly at them and gave a nervous little laugh that sounded more like a tiny cough.

"And our owners let us sleep in their soft beds with them every night," continued Soupy.

"What's a 'bed?,'" asked Beau.

"Oh, it's a big, soft place to sleep. It's much better than sleeping in the forest," said Soupy, remembering when he lived in the forest raising Ferdinand. It had taken some time getting used to sleeping inside the hard, lumpy log.

"That does sound nice," said Beau.

"And even in the winter when it's freezing out-side, it's nice and warm in our houses," said Puff Puff.

"Ah, that's why you all have the tips of your ears and your tails. Last winter, it was so cold that my tail and ears hurt real bad. But later, I couldn't feel them at all," explained Beau. "And then a cou-ple days later, they were gone."

The cats nodded sympathetically.

"But you are still *beautimous*, Beau!," said Lola enthusiastically.

Beau looked at Lola and giggled.

"Oh, and when it's raining and lightening out-side, it's quiet and dry inside our houses," said Soupy.

"Really?," asked Beau. She hated storms. She and her kittens were always very frightened and wet during storms. "Living in houses *does* sound nice." She looked across the field toward the hous-es.

"You can come inside our house to see what it's like some time, Beau," invited Puff Puff.

Spider Man said, "You could come tomorrow and see how soft a bed is."

Beau bit her lip nervously.

"Our Cindy and Steve will be at work all day," said Lola.

Beau didn't like this idea but she saw everyone looking at her, waiting for her answer.

"Um, I guess I could run in real fast and see the 'bed' and then leave," offered Beau.

"Good," said Lila. "We'll come and get you tomorrow morning and we'll all go into our house."

Beau mustered up a little smile for them.

Now that their plan for Beau to go into Lila and Lola's house tomorrow was set, Soupy changed the subject. "I'm gonna go look for Ferdinand." And with that, he ran off into the forest.

This time, Soupy ran around the entire outer boundary of the forest calling for Ferdinand but no one answered. He stopped to catch his breath and sighed heavily. Next, he ran in a smaller circle inside the forest calling "FERDINAAAAND! FERRR... DI...NAAAAAAND!" No one answered.

Where is he? I hope he's okay. Soupy rejoined the other cats and kittens disheartened.

When the other cats saw Soupy returning, they stood up and quickly looked behind him, hoping to see a big raccoon following him.

Soupy shook his head. "I couldn't find him," he said sadly.

"Poor Soup," said Spider Man. He patted Soupy's shoulder.

"You'll find him tomorrow, I bet," said Puff Puff.

Lila and Lola just looked at Soupy and nodded quickly.

Soupy laid down in the grass and closed his eyes wearily.

Chapter 7
Beau Visits a House

The next day, everyone reached Beau and her babies at about 8:30 a.m. She was very happy to see them but a little nervous about their plan to visit Lila and Lola's house to see what a bed was like.

"Hi, guys," said Beau.

Soupy plopped a piece of bacon at Beau's feet, Spider Man placed half of a grilled cheese sandwich that his Marcy had left on her plate that morning, and Lila and Lola also had big pieces of bacon in their mouths for Beau. Cindy had made extra so that Lila and Lola could bring some to their friend.

"Oh thank you!," said Beau, her eyes almost popping out of her head at the feast they had brought her. She quickly started crunching on the bacon.

The other cats played with the kittens while Beau gobbled up her breakfast.

"Hi Squeaky!," said Puff Puff, smiling. Puff Puff loved both babies, but Squeaky was his favorite. Squeaky answered him by scurrying over and smacking him in the face. Puff Puff chuckled and licked her head. Squeaky crouched down, secured her back legs' footing in the ground, causing her little bottom to wiggle back and forth, and then pounced on Puff Puff's head. Puff Puff grabbed Squeaky with his paw and washed her face while she wiggled to get away so she could pounce on him again.

Spider Man looked at Hoppy and laid down in the grass. As soon as little Hoppy saw Spider Man lay down, his eyes widened in excitement. He hopped over to Spider Man as fast as he could, hopped onto his stomach, and bit his shoulder. Spider Man laughed. Hoppy liked hopping up and down on Spider Man's stomach because it was so big and soft.

They all played like this for a while, allowing Beau's food to digest.

Lila finally said, "Well, Beau, are you ready to go to our house?"

Beau didn't want to, but everyone was looking at her expectantly. She scratched her side.

"Okay," she said quietly. She wanted to ask if they could postpone the trip until tomorrow but she didn't want them to think she was a scaredy-cat. She scratched her ear.

"It'll be okay," assured Lola.

"I'll stay here and watch the kittens," volunteered Spider Man, not wanting to have to run the distance home again.

So Lila, Lola, Soupy, Puff Puff, and Beau jogged toward the houses and within a few minutes, they were approaching Lila and Lola's house. But the closer they got to the house, the slower Beau ran. Then she was only walking. Soupy noticed her lagging behind. He turned and walked back to Beau.

"What's wrong?"

The other cats stopped and looked back at Beau. They ran back to her, too.

She looked at them apologetically.

"Are you sure no one is home?" Beau looked at the house nervously. She was feeling a little sick to her stomach.

"Yes, we saw them drive off for work this morning," said Lola.

Beau sighed and began walking toward the houses again. The little herd of cats walked through the picket fence and were in Lila and Lola's back yard. They approached the cat door and Lila went inside through the flap. She held the flap open for the other cats with her head. Lola walked into the kitchen through the door, too, and looked out at Beau.

Beau gulped and cautiously walked through the cat door. She looked around at the kitchen. She stood perfectly still and quiet, listening. The other cats stood still, too, so she could hear that Cindy and Steve weren't home. When she was sure they were alone, she looked at Lila and Lola's bowl of water.

Lola saw Beau looking at the water and said, "Go ahead. Drink. You must be thirsty."

Eating three pieces of salty bacon had made Beau thirsty. She drank for a long time from the fresh bowl of water.

Lila said, "Okay, ready to go upstairs and see the bed, Beau?"

Beau took a slow deep breath to gather her strength and nodded.

"Follow us," said Lila as she slowly walked out of the kitchen, down the hall, and up the stairs.

Beau looked around at the big house nervously as she followed Lila. The cats climbed the stairs to the second floor in a single file. Lola looked behind her to make sure Beau was still following. Beau looked very nervous, so Lola gave her a big reassuring smile. But Beau couldn't muster up a smile for Lola right then. They reached the landing to the second floor where there were four doors; one leading to a bathroom and three leading to bedrooms. Lola walked into the master bedroom and Beau slowly followed her. The other cats entered the room, too. The house was very quiet.

"Here it is," said Lila, pointing to the big queen-size bed. She jumped onto the bed.

Soupy jumped up on the bed, too, and looked down at Beau. "Come on up, Beau." He smiled down at her.

Beau approached the bed cautiously and smelled the dust ruffle. Puff Puff and Lola jumped up on the bed and the four cats looked down at Beau.

"It's nice and soft," said Puff Puff. He plopped down on the bed and stretched.

If tiny Puff Puff can do it, then so can I! Beau jumped up on the bed finally.

"Wow! It IS soft!," she said. She sniffed the blankets.

"Come over here and try this out," said Lola. "*This* is a pillow. It's even more softer than the bed!" Lola sat on one of the pillows.

Beau looked all around. She was still nervous but she walked to the other big fluffy pillow and stepped on it. She went into a trance for a minute while rhythmically kneading the pillow with her two front paws as if it were a ball of pizza dough. Then she blissfully plopped down on it.

"Soft," she said dreamily as she closed her eyes and arched her whole body and stretched.

"If you had a owner, you could sleep in one of these every night," said Soupy.

"This is much more better than sleeping in the forest," said Beau. The hard ground and sticks and rocks always dug into her bony little body.

Cindy was a talented decorator and loved vibrant colors. She had decorated their bedroom in rich, deep greens and blues. The drapes were a beautiful floral pattern. Beau felt very at home there as if she were still in the forest, except everything was soft and peaceful.

The telephone on the nightstand rang loudly. Beau screeched and hissed in horror and immediately dashed out of the room, down the stairs, and out the cat door like lightening, her heart pounding in her chest.

"OH NO!," gasped Lila.

"WAIT, BEAU! IT'S JUST THE PHONE," called Soupy after her.

All the cats ran after Beau as fast as they could. Soupy reached the cat door first and dashed outside after Beau. Lila and Lola tried to run through the cat door at the exact same time and became stuck there together for a moment.

"OOFF!" They looked at each other with annoyed expressions and growled.

Lola pulled back and let Lila go first.

Beau was about ten yards ahead of the group still running as fast as she could toward the forest.

"BEAU, WAIT!," screamed Soupy.

"WAIT, BEAU!," screamed Lila.

Beau heard their screams and slowed down a little. She looked over her shoulder to see if the monster that had made that horrible noise in the bedroom was also chasing her but she only saw the cats. She stopped to catch her breath.

When they caught up to Beau, she exclaimed, "Oh my gosh!" Her chest was heaving. "What WAS that...that *noise*?!"

Puff Puff said, "That was just a phone, Beau. That's all." He was out of breath.

"A...'phone?,'" Beau looked toward Lila and Lola's house fearfully.

"A phone is just for humans to talk to each other," explained Lila.

"And...and...it makes that horrible sound when someone wants to talk to your owners?!," asked Beau, grimacing.

"Right, when the phone 'rings,' humans pick it up and talk to each other," explained Soupy.

"You don't have to be ascared of a phone," said Lola.

"It was so loud!"

"It IS loud," agreed Lola, nodding.

"It's okay, Beau," said Puff Puff. "The first few times I heard a phone ring, I ran, too!"

Beau smiled at Puff Puff gratefully.

"Well," said Soupy. "That's probably enough house-exploring for one day."

"Let's go back to your kittens," said Lila.

Chapter 8
A Very, *Very* Big Bird!

Puff Puff had always wished he could be a father. The moment he set eyes on the kittens, he loved them as if they were his own. The next day when the cats were on their way to visit Beau and her babies, while crossing the field, they noticed a very large bird flying in the sky, slowly gliding over the field with its wings outstretched. Beau was laying down at the forest's edge washing her paws and face. Tiny Squeaky and Hoppy were wrestling and chasing each other nearby in the field.

The large raptor was hungry. He slowly circled the field looking for breakfast. With his keen eyes, he was able to see small animals in the grass from very long distances. Toward his right near the forest, he spotted two tiny animals moving on the ground and a bigger animal lying right at the forest's edge, probably the smaller ones' mother. The hawk turned toward Squeaky and Hoppy.

The cats could see Beau and her babies from across the field, but they put their food on the ground to catch their breath for a moment before continuing.

"Wow, that's the biggest bird I've ever seen!," remarked little Lola, looking up at the sky.

"Jeepers creepers, it sure is!," said Puff Puff, thinking that the bird might even be bigger than he was!

Puff Puff thought about a day long ago when he saw a huge bird like that try to catch a squirrel. The squirrel had barely escaped from the bird by dashing into a nearby shrub. Puff Puff remembered the bird's big sharp claws and sharp beak. The kittens were even smaller than the squirrel. Puff Puff gasped loudly!

"MY KITTENS!," he screeched! "IT WANTS TO EAT MY KITTENS!" Puff Puff bolted across the field toward the kittens at lightening speed!

The other cats gasped and ran toward the kittens, too. Beau heard Puff Puff screaming but couldn't understand what he said because he was across the field. But she instinctively stood up and darted toward her babies, terrified! She saw all the cats running like lightening toward her kittens. She loved her kittens from the bottom of her heart and knew that they were small and helpless. She scanned the field for an approaching dog as she ran but couldn't see any. She looked at the other cats then and saw them looking up. She looked up, too, and saw it!

Beau let out a blood-curdling scream!

A huge bird with a sharp beak and long sharp talons on its feet was diving through the air right toward her babies!

Hoppy and Squeaky heard Puff Puff's scream and now their mother's and stopped wrestling. They scrambled to their feet in a panic and ran toward their mother as fast as their short little legs would carry them, which wasn't very fast.

The raptor saw the small herd of animals dashing toward the babies, probably to protect them from him. He knew then that he had to hurry or he would miss his breakfast. The babies were running toward their mother now. He scoffed at how slowly they ran. But the timing was going to be close. The smaller white animal was ahead of the rest of the pack and for a second, the hawk considered making a tasty meal out of him instead of one of the babies. But the tiny animal was curling his lips and he could see his fangs. His sharp claws grasped the ground as he ran at lightening speed. It was also growling and screaming and looking right into the hawk's eyes. The hawk frowned. Even though the white animal was small, it seemed impressively vicious. The tiny thing had an insane look in his eyes, too, that actually made the raptor nervous. He sensed that the tiny fluff-ball would fight to the death to protect those babies, and in the second or two that he spent fighting with it, the other animals could catch up to him and overtake him. At the last second when the raptor was almost upon the kittens, he made a quick turn upward toward the sky again. He decided to fly over the forest to see if he could find some other unsuspecting victim drinking from the creek for his breakfast instead. As he flew away, he saw that the tiny white animal was still growling ferociously and was actually running after him on the ground directly below him.

The hawk sneered at the fluffy animal resentfully. *You must be rabid!* But he flew faster toward the forest.

All the cats and the kittens came together then, out of breath. The kittens hid under their momma, shaking in fear. They had never heard their mother scream before.

"Quick!," said Lila. "Into the forest! Everyone!" She looked up at the sky fearfully, while pushing the group toward the forest.

Spider Man grabbed Hoppy by the scruff of the neck and Beau picked up Squeaky and they all ran toward the forest, gaping up at the sky, terrified that the monster bird would return.

When they were all safely hidden in the brush, Lila and Lola stood there for a minute trying to catch their breath. Poor chubby Spider Man laid down and gasped for air.

Puff Puff returned to the group after making sure that the bird would not return and he quickly went to each kitten to make sure they were all right. He licked each kitten's head and cooed, "It's okay now. You're okay." Squeaky and Hoppy relaxed and began to purr when Puff Puff did this. Beau just laid next to her babies out of breath and in shock. She looked around at all of them emotionally.

"Thank you! Thank you all for saving my kittens!" Beau hadn't noticed the huge bird in the sky because she was busy taking a bath. She shuddered to think of what would've happened if her new friends hadn't shown up exactly when they did.

"Don't be redikerous," said little Lola breathlessly.

Puff Puff continued licking the kittens' heads and faces to assure himself they were okay. That had been a very close call...too close. The kittens started to wrestle with each other again. Then Hoppy saw Spider Man laying on the ground, so he ran up to him and hopped onto his stomach.

Hoppy kneaded Spider Man's soft belly and purred. Spider Man smiled and closed his eyes gratefully.

Lila slowly looked over at Puff Puff and stared at him as if seeing him for the very first time. Lola stared at Puff Puff, too, in amazement. Spider Man was silently staring at little Puff Puff, as well. It was completely out of character for their tiny Puff Puff to act so bravely; running full speed ahead directly at a huge predatory bird that could have easily carried *him* off and eaten *him*. Their tiny friend was usually afraid of his own shadow.

Lila wanted to praise Puff Puff for being so brave but she was afraid that it would bring attention to the fact that he was usually so *timid*. So she decided not to say anything at all.

Soupy abruptly declared, "Beau! You have to move your family under my porch!"

Everyone turned toward Soupy.

"You and the kittens aren't safe out here, Beau!," said Puff Puff, shaking his head.

Squeaky crawled onto Beau's shoulder and bit her ear and shook it viciously. Beau didn't want to move closer to the houses but she felt unsafe now living where they were. She frowned, trying to decide what to do.

"Beau, that monster bird is going to come back for your kittens, you know," said Puff Puff.

Beau twirled around to look at Puff Puff. There was great fear in his eyes. She looked up at the sky again, wide-eyed.

Spider Man volunteered, "I'll carry Hoppy."

"I'll carry Squeaky!," declared Puff Puff.

Still Beau didn't move and looked very uneasy.

"You would be closer to our bowls of food if you lived under my porch," coaxed Soupy.

Beau's mouth watered.

"No one has to know that you're living there," cajoled Lola.

Spider Man thought about how nice it would be not to have to make the long three block trip to visit Beau and her kittens every day.

"And the spaces between the wooden slates under the porch are too small for a dog to get through," said Lila.

"Really?," asked Beau. Beau always worried about dogs getting her kittens.

"Well, who else lives with you, Soupy? Any monsters...I mean *humans* who might chase me with a big stick or shoot me?," asked Beau, looking skeptically at Soupy.

"No!," said Soupy. "My Molly is very beautimous and the nicest human-kitten in the world. She has a father and a brother but they wouldn't hurt you or your kittens either," promised Soupy.

Lila, Lola, and Spider Man all nodded at Beau.

Beau didn't like change. She had always lived in the forest, first with her mother, then with Shmoopy, Bopey, and Mopey, and now with her kittens. But she knew she had to do this for the safety of her kittens. She would do anything for them.

Beau frowned and looked into the forest and hoped that Shmoopy, Bopey, and Mopey would follow. She didn't want them thinking that she just abandoned them for no reason.

Beau was silent for a moment, just looking at Soupy. "Well…I guess we better move under your porch then." She nodded just once.

"Yaaaaay!," cheered Puff Puff, relieved that his kittens would be safe from the huge bird.

"Okay, let's go!," said Spider Man.

"What?! Now?!," said Beau with her mouth hanging open.

"Yes! The sooner the better. Who knows when that monster bird will come back!," said Lila.

Beau looked up at the sky fearfully and placed her arms over her kittens. When she didn't see the bird, she stood up.

"Let's go!," she said.

The kittens clamored around Beau's legs, a little frightened, not understanding what was happening. Spider Man picked up Hoppy by the scruff of the neck and Puff Puff picked up Squeaky and everyone ran toward the houses together. Lila and Lola kept a watch on the sky above.

When they had run about 30 feet, Beau looked back toward the forest, worried about her three friends. But she saw them standing there together at the edge of the forest, smiling at her.

"Go on, Beau. We'll find you. Don't worry," yelled Shmoopy.

"You just keep your babies safe from that monster!," yelled Mopey, pointing up at the sky.

Bopey looked up at the sky fearfully and held onto Shmoopy's and Mopey's tails, ready to yank them back into the forest if the killer bird appeared again.

Beau smiled, relieved that they knew what was happening.

"Okay!" Beau waved goodbye to her friends. "Bye for now!"

Lola saw Beau do this and curiously looked back toward the forest to see who she was talking to. Lola couldn't see anyone, so she assumed Beau was simply saying goodbye to the forest.

All the cats took turns carrying the chubby kittens and they arrived at Soupy's house in six minutes.

Soupy pointed at the porch and the criss-crossed wooden slats on the side. "Here it is."

Soupy squeezed through an opening between the slats and went underneath the porch. Beau peeked inside and liked what she saw. It was sheltered and shaded. She crawled through the slats and the kittens quickly followed her and clamored around her legs again, nervous about their new surroundings. Beau laid down and the kittens snuggled against her for comfort. She licked their heads and faces.

"Now we don't have to make the trip to the forest to bring you food any more, Beau," said Spider Man, peeking through the slats. He didn't go through the slats because he wasn't sure he would fit.

Soupy hung his head sadly. Spider Man looked at him and realized his thoughtless mistake! "Oh! Except for when we go to look for Ferdinand with Soupy!"

Soupy lifted his head and smiled at Spider Man.

"We'll find him, Soup!," assured Puff Puff.

Chapter 9
Meeting Molly

The next morning, while Beau was eating the bacon and ham that her friends brought her, Lila brought up a difficult subject.

"I've been thinking, Beau," she said.

Beau looked at Lila. "About what?," she asked with her mouth full of bacon.

"Well, we're going to have to find homes for your babies. They can't live under Soupy's porch forever."

Beau's gasped! "Why not?!"

All the cats looked at Lila.

"Well, when winter comes, it's gonna be freezing again. You don't want the babies' ears to freeze off, do you?," asked Lila.

Beau stopped eating. "No!," she said! She thought of her ears without their tips and how Princess made fun of them.

"Well then we have to find the babies warm homes to live in," said Lila.

Everyone looked at Beau and nodded encouragingly.

Beau gulped. "With…with *humans*?!"

"Yes, with nice people who will feed them every day and let them sleep in their soft beds with them every night."

Beau blinked several times silently and continued chewing slowly.

"Hey!," said Puff Puff, his nostrils flaring. "Maybe my Carli's mom will let Squeaky move in with us!" Puff Puff stood up and shifted quickly from paw to paw excitedly.

"Oh! And maybe my Marcy will take Hoppy!," said Spider Man breathlessly.

Beau scratched her ear feverishly.

"I have a idea!," said Lola. Everyone looked at Lola. "How 'bout we start off slowly? We introduce Beau to little Molly. Molly's so sweet. You're gonna just love her, Beau!"

Beau looked at her kittens fearfully.

"So, what do you say, Beau? Do you want to meet my Molly?," asked Soupy, with raised eyebrows.

Beau wished the cats wouldn't rush her into everything. "C' .. can I think about it for a few days?"

"I don't want to rush you, Beau, but the sooner your babies meet a human, the less ascared they'll be of them," explained Lila. Everyone nodded at Beau.

Beau sighed. "How 'bout tomorrow?"

"Yes! Tomorrow!," said Soupy.

✸ ✸ ✸

The next day when Billy got off the bus and ran into the house, Soupy did not run in after him. Instead, he waited in the lilac bushes in front of the porch for Molly. When she walked up to the stairs to the porch, Soupy walked out of the bushes right in front of her. Molly's eyes opened very wide!

"Soupy!," she gasped! "What?! How did you get outside?!" Soupy rubbed against her legs.

"Oh my gosh!" Molly bent down to pick Soupy up, but he darted to the side of the porch by the wooden slats.

"Soupy, no! Come here!"

Molly was terrified that Soupy would get lost again but Soupy stopped running right by the side of the porch and looked back at her. Molly scurried over to Soupy, trying not to scare him. But when she got close to him again, he climbed through the slats on the side of the porch.

"Soupy! Don't go in there!" Molly crouched down and fearfully peered through the slats.

"Souuuuuuupy," Molly cajoled. "Please come to Mommy, sweetheart." She put her arm through the slats and held out her dirty little hand toward him. Her eyes adjusted to the deep shade under the porch and she realized she was looking at a new cat and two kittens. All three of them hissed at her in unison.

"Oh!," she gasped. "Soupy! There's a little family living under the porch!"

Beau sat by her kittens very afraid. She hissed at Molly again.

"Oh! Don't be ascared, kitty," said Molly. "I won't hurt you."

Beau relaxed a little but gave Molly another warning hiss anyway. She noticed that Molly was much smaller than the boy who shot her and the woman who had chased her with the stick.

"Oh!" Molly had an idea. She ran into the house. Spider Man, Puff Puff, Lola, and Lila gathered around the side of the porch, too, watching.

Beau was breathing heavily, very nervous at being so close to a human.

"See how nice she is, Beau?," said Puff Puff hopefully.

"She does seem nice," admitted Beau.

Squeaky jumped up and bit Beau's cheek. Hoppy took a hold of Beau's short tail with his tiny teeth and shook it viciously.

The cats heard Molly rushing out the front door and down the steps. She scurried over to the side of the porch again and held something out to Beau through the slats. It smelled scrumptious. It was a chunk of liver sausage. Beau's mouth watered. Even the kittens were cautiously walking toward the heavenly smell. Molly stayed very still.

"No, babies!," warned Beau but they kept walking toward the smell.

"It's okay, kittens. Come and get it," cooed Molly.

"She won't hurt them, Beau," said Soupy. Beau was frozen with fright as she watched her babies slowly approach the little ugly Molly monster.

Squeaky reached Molly's hand first and she smelled the liver sausage curiously. She took a little lick. It was very good. She took a tiny bite. Hoppy hopped over to the liver sausage now and licked it a couple of times, too. Beau held her breath! Both kittens were taking tiny bites of the sausage and it quickly disappeared. They licked Molly's fingers when the sausage was gone.

"Sweet babies," said Molly quietly, barely able to contain her excitement. Molly adored kittens. "I'll go get more." She got up slowly so she didn't scare the kittens and went into the house to get more sausage.

"See, Beau?! We told you Molly was nice!," said Lola, bouncing up and down.

Beau looked at Lola and nodded nervously.

"Why don't you take a little bite of the food this time," encouraged Spider Man.

"Oh! I uh...I'm not hungry." She closed her eyes and quickly shook her head.

The rest of the cats exchanged looks. They knew this wasn't true.

"Oh, come on, Beau. You can do it!," coached Puff Puff.

"You can do it! You can do it!," all the cats chanted together like a team of little furry cheerleaders.

Beau giggled. "Oh, all right. I'll try."

"Yaaay!," cheered everyone.

Molly arrived at the side of the porch again and held out more liver sausage to Beau. The kittens scurried over to Molly again and started taking tiny bites of the sausage. Molly had another chunk of sausage in her other hand reserved just for Beau.

"Go on, Beau!," whispered Spider Man.

"Go on!," urged Lila and Lola in unison.

"Okay! Okay!," said Beau. She slowly took a step closer to Molly. Then another.

"Come on, sweetheart," Molly cooed softly at Beau. Beau licked her lips. The liver sausage smelled heavenly.

Very, very slowly Beau crept up to Molly. When she was close enough, she stretched out her neck and nervously took a tiny bite while watching Molly closely. It was delicious. Beau took another bite and another, never taking her eyes off Molly. Molly knew the Momma cat was very scared, so she remained perfectly still. When the liver was gone, Beau immediately retreated to the far corner of the sub-porch area to watch Molly wearily again. She bathed herself and her kittens.

"Good girl!," said Molly softly. Molly thought that the cat must have had a very difficult life, because she only had one eye and a foot that stuck straight out from her ankle. Beau feverishly scratched behind her ears.

"Poor baby, you must have fleas, too," said Molly sadly. At that moment, Beau met Molly's eyes with her eye. They stared into each other's eyes and they recognized something. Molly smiled at Beau and Beau became very calm then. Both Molly and Beau had suffered greatly because of their appearances. Molly was teased constantly by the other children. And Beau had been teased mercilessly by Princess for her ragged appearance. An understanding passed between Molly and Beau. Molly held out the second chuck of liver sausage for Beau and this time, Beau walked quickly to Molly and started eating the sausage out of her hand.

"Good girl! We need to fatten you up," said Molly. She reached out and stroked the top of Beau's head. This startled Beau and she hissed at her!

"Oh! Sorry!," whispered Molly. She remained very still again and slowly Beau relaxed and once again started eating the liver sausage. Molly softly stroked Beau's head with just her pointer finger this time when she was pre-occupied with eating the tasty sausage. Beau was more interested in eating than hissing, so Molly kept stroking her head. The liver sausage was gone now, but Beau stayed put and allowed Molly to stroke her head.

"This feels kind of good," said Beau to the other cats. "What's she doing?"

"She's 'petting' you!," explained Puff Puff.

"Ah," said Beau. To her surprise, she heard herself purring.

Molly reached out and petted tiny Squeaky next. "Hi, baby," cooed Molly. Squeaky squeaked at Molly and Molly giggled. She scratched Squeaky under her little chin softly and she began to purr. She petted Hoppy next and both kittens seemed to accept Molly's touch. Beau watched fearfully but soon grew confident that Molly wouldn't hurt her babies.

The kittens started grabbing Molly's fingers and biting them playfully.

"Oooh! You *got* me!," said Molly, laughing softly. She picked up tiny Hoppy and lifted him through the slats. Beau scurried up to the slats.

"MEOW! MEOW!," yelled Beau loudly. (Translation: "What are you doing?! You put my baby down right now!)

"It's okay, Momma kitty. I would never hurt your baby!," assured Molly. She kissed Hoppy and snuggled him and Hoppy purred loudly and slapped Molly on the nose. Beau heard her tiny son purring and she relaxed. Molly picked up each kitten in turn and kissed them and snuggled them and they both purred loudly.

"Well! I better go get you some food and water, Momma!" Off ran Molly again. She returned a few minutes later with a big bowl of cold, fresh water, and a big bowl of hard cat food. She carefully put them through the slats on the ground under the porch. She then ran back inside the house and returned with another bowl, this time full of canned cat food that she also placed inside the wooden slats. The wet food smelled delicious, so Beau and the kittens scurried up to the bowl and started eating. Beau looked up at Molly every few seconds.

While Beau and her babies ate, Molly got up and ran over to Marcy's house next door. Marcy loved Molly as much as she loved her own grandchildren. And since Molly's mother left her father for another man last fall, Marcy was even more concerned for Molly's well-being. Molly knew that Marcy would know what to do about the little family living under her porch. Molly quickly opened Marcy's front door and ran into the kitchen where Marcy was stirring a big pot on the stove that smelled delicious.

"Hi, sweetie!," said Marcy warmly. Marcy always left the door open for Molly to come and go as she pleased. "I'm making your favorite, chicken noodle soup."

"Hurry, Marcy!" Molly motioned for Marcy to follow her. "There's a Momma cat and two kittens living under my porch!"

"Oh! Really?!," said Marcy.

"Yeah! Come on!"

"Oh my gosh!" Marcy quickly wiped her hands on a towel and followed Molly.

"But you have to be very quiet 'cause the Momma cat is ascared," said Molly as she scurried back to her porch. Marcy trotted as fast as she could behind Molly, trying her best in her 52-year-old body to keep up with the little 7-year-old.

"I'll be quiet," whispered Marcy. "Maybe she's a feral cat?"

"What does 'feral' mean," asked Molly. She stopped to look up at Marcy.

"It's a cat that was born outside in the wild. They're very afraid of humans because they think we're their predators. They actually think we want to eat them," explained Marcy.

Molly looked at Marcy wide-eyed. "Oh!," she said simply and started walking briskly toward her porch again. When they got closer to the porch, Molly slowed down and then crouched down by the wooden slats. Marcy did the same. They both peered through the slats under the porch. This time, Beau and the kittens sat perfectly still, afraid of this larger newcomer human.

After a moment when Marcy's eyes adjusted to the deep shade under the porch, she saw the adorable family and cooed softly to them, "Hi, guys." Marcy smiled from ear to ear. In her head, she was already planning what she was going to do to help the little family. Marcy could see how horribly thin the mother was.

"What's wrong with her face?"

"She only has one eye," explained Molly matter-of-factly.

"Oh!," said Marcy softly. "Poor little girl!"

Molly recognized the sadness in Marcy's voice, so she patted her shoulder.

Then Marcy noticed Beau's foot sticking out at a 90 degree angle from her leg.

"Oh, no! Look at her foot!," said Marcy.

Molly had seen that the momma cat didn't favor her foot at all. Beau's broken ankle had healed a long time ago and although it was a little scary-looking, it actually caused Beau no pain now and she walked on it as if nothing had ever happened to it.

"It doesn't hurt her any more," assured Molly matter-of-factly.

"No?," asked Marcy, looking at Molly.

"No," Molly shook her head. "She walks on it just fine."

"What a rough life you've had," said Marcy sadly. "But we're gonna help them now, right, Molly?"

Molly looked up into Marcy's beautiful face and smiled gratefully at her. "Right!" She nodded her head just once.

Marcy sniffled.

"So what are we gonna do?," asked Molly with great hope in her voice.

"Oh...well, we're gonna find them good homes!," declared Marcy with absolute certainty.

Molly's smile spread as wide as it could across her dirty little face.

"Maybe Carli will want a kitten," offered Molly, trying to think of a "good" home.

Puff Puff stood up quickly. *My own kitten!* His eyes darted back and forth at this exciting thought. A grasshopper hopped past Puff Puff and he quickly chased after it.

"Oh, good idea!," said Marcy.

"OH!," gasped Molly as she clasped her hands together under her chin. "Maybe *my* Daddy will let *me* keep one!" Molly smiled from ear to ear, and her nostrils flared at this wonderful thought.

"Well…maybe," said Marcy uneasily. She knew that Molly's father was struggling financially.

"We need to be tricky, though" said Marcy.

"What do you mean?," whispered Molly, looking intently into Marcy's face.

"If we bring a kitten *with* us when we ask people if they want one, they'll be much more likely to say 'yes' because of how *cute* they are."

"Oh!," giggled Molly. "That IS tricky!"

"The kittens look like they are about seven or eight weeks old now," said Marcy. "So they should be ready to be taken away from their Momma soon."

The can of cat food was all gone now and Beau was licking her kittens clean while watching Marcy suspiciously.

Beau looked at the other cats. "I don't like this," she said, frowning.

"Maybe Molly and Marcy will be able to find homes for the kittens very close by so you can still see them every day," said Lila.

Beau's frown went away.

"Also," said little Lola. "Remember how cold it gets in the winter? You don't want your babies to freeze all winter, do you?"

Beau shook her head quickly. "You're right. They need to find warm houses to live in so their ears and tails don't...end up looking like mine."

"I like your ears!," said Spider Man, gesturing toward Beau's ears.

Beau looked at Spider Man quickly, surprised. "You do?!" She didn't quite believe him.

Spider Man nodded enthusiastically. "Yes!," he assured her. "Yes I do!" He gave one big nod of his head to emphasize his point.

"Me, too!," declared Puff Puff. "I get tired of looking at the same old pointy ears all the time."

Beau giggled.

Chapter 10
A Happy Home for Hoppy

The next morning, Marcy brought fresh water and two large bowls filled with canned cat food for Beau and her babies. She quietly put them through the slats under the porch while cooing softly to them. The babies quickly ran up to the bowls and started eating. Beau watched Marcy suspiciously for a minute before cautiously walking up to the food. Marcy watched the adorable kittens and the ragged, skeletal momma cat eat for a few minutes before going home to put a load of laundry in and go shopping.

I need to stock up on cat food!

When Molly came home from camp, she again found Soupy waiting for her by the steps of the porch along with Spider Man, Puff Puff, Lila, and Lola.

"Soupy!," exclaimed Molly. "How do you keep getting out of the house?!" She scurried over to the side of the porch and peered through the slats and saw Beau and her babies snuggling together in one of Spider Man's extra large cat beds that Marcy squeezed through the slats for them earlier.

"Hi, kitties," said Molly softly, smiling. To her great delight, the kittens quickly climbed out of the bed and crawled through the slats and into her lap. Molly was in heaven.

Beau instinctively wanted to follow her babies and took a few steps closer to Molly. The kittens purred and dug their tiny sharp claws into Molly's shirt and climbed up to her shoulders, scratching her a little. Hoppy started biting Molly's scraggly hair. Squeaky scratched Molly's cheek playfully and bit her ear. Molly giggled.

Marcy had heard the camp bus come and go, so she came over to Molly by the porch.

"Hi!," said Marcy cheerily. "I brought them two cans of cat food this morning and gave them one of Spider Man's beds."

"I see," said Molly. "So should I bring a kitten over to Carli's house to see if her mom will let her keep it?"

"Yes! The sooner we get these babies a home and a check-up at the vet's, the better."

"I'll go right now!"

"I'll wait here for you. I don't want Carli's mom to know that I'm in cahoots with you."

"Okay, here, hold this kitten," instructed Molly as she handed Hoppy to Marcy. "I love both babies, but I eckspecially love this one 'cause he hops everywhere like a little bunny-rabbit!"

Marcy chuckled and took Hoppy from Molly. Molly held Squeaky snugly as she stood up.

"Good luck!," said Marcy. Molly smiled at Marcy as she walked toward her friend's house.

Molly cooed softly to Squeaky as she walked so she wouldn't be scared. She rang Carli's doorbell and waited anxiously, hoping that it would be Carli who answered the door, not her mother. Molly heard fast running up to the door from inside and knew it was Carli. Mrs. Adler didn't run. Carli peered through the glass panel on the side of the door and saw Molly. Carli smiled at her messy little best friend. Then she noticed that she was holding a kitten and her eyes almost popped out of her head. Molly giggled softly.

Carli swung the door wide open and said, "A kitten?!"

"Shshshsh! Don't ascare her, Carli!," said Molly crossly.

"Come in! Come in!," whispered Carli, excitedly motioning for Molly to enter the house.

"She's so cute! Where'd you get 'er?!" She took the kitten from Molly. Squeaky squeaked at Carli fearfully.

"It's okay, baby," assured Carli softly. Squeaky grabbed a lock of Carli's brown hair and bit it. Carli giggled and wiggled her hair for Squeaky. She grabbed it with both paws and bit it harder.

"Oh, she's so soft. I love her! Can I keep her?," asked Carli looking pleadingly at Molly. "Or is she yours?," she asked sadly.

"No, she's not mine. She lives under my porch with her mom and one other kitten."

"I wanna see! But let me ask my mom if I can keep this kitten first."

"K," answered Molly, crossing her fingers behind her back.

The girls walked into the kitchen where Mrs. Adler was preparing dinner. She turned and saw Molly.

"Hi, Miss Molly! How are you?"

She saw the adorable kitten in her daughter's hands then and didn't wait for an answer from Molly.

"A baby!," she exclaimed. She quickly wiped her hands on a dish towel and started petting the kitten's little head. Squeaky hissed at Mrs. Adler.

"Oh!," she laughed. "It's all right, honey," she said, while taking Squeaky from Carli. She petted her tiny head and scratched under her chin and Squeaky calmed down and purred. "Oh my goodness, she's just the cutest little thing in the world! Is she yours, Molly?"

"Um, no, she's not mine. She just lives under my porch."

"Under your porch?!" Mrs. Adler frowned.

"Yes, with her Momma and one other kitten."

"Oooh, poor little family."

"Can I keep 'er, Mom?! Can I keep 'er? Please?! Pleeeeeeeeease!?," whined Carli.

"Oh, honey," Mrs. Adler frowned. "I don't know about that."

"Oooooooh!" Carli skewed up her face in horrible frustration. Her "Oooooooh" became louder and louder as it went on.

Her mother saw one of Carli's spoiled temper tantrums coming on and quickly interrupted her. "I have to talk to your father first, Carli!" She almost had to yell to be heard over Carli.

"When's he coming home?!," demanded Carli, clasping her hands together under her chin.

"He should be home soon. Molly, can we keep the kitten here to show Carli's dad? I think if he sees how cute she is, we might have a better chance of him letting us keep her."

"Sure!"

Carli hugged her mom around the waist. "I love you, Mom!"

"Yeah, yeah," she said while she kissed the tiny kitten. The kitten squeaked and slapped her across the nose.

"Oh!," gasped Mrs. Adler.

"Giver 'er back to me!," said Carli bossily, taking the kitten out of her mother's hands.

"Fine!," said Carli's mom, resentfully. She wanted to continue playing with the adorable kitten herself, but she had to get dinner ready anyway.

"Luckily," said Mrs. Adler, holding her pointer finger up, "I'm making spaghetti, your father's favorite, so hopefully that'll put him in a good mood and more likely to say 'yes' to keeping the kitten."

Carli held Squeaky up against her cheek in one hand and crossed her fingers for good luck with the other hand.

"Do you want to eat over, Molly?," asked Mrs. Adler.

"No, thank you. I don't like puhsketti." Molly shook her head.

Mrs. Adler laughed. "Well, I guess if you don't like 'puhsketti,' then you just don't like puhsketti!"

Molly suspected that Carli's mom might be teasing her about something but she wasn't sure, so she just smiled politely at her.

"Now you girls go into the TV room with the kitten. I'll talk to your father first and then bring him in to see the kitten."

"Okay," said Carli. She and Molly went into the TV room together with Squeaky.

Mrs. Adler looked at the clock and put a piece of garlic bread in the oven. Then she went into the washroom to touch up her makeup.

Ten minutes later, Mr. Adler came home. As soon as he opened the door, he smelled the garlic bread and spaghetti sauce and inhaled deeply, smiling. He laid his briefcase down on the hallway table and walked into the kitchen.

"Mmmm. My favorite!"

Mrs. Adler was stirring the sauce, so he kissed her quickly on the cheek.

"How was your day, honey?," she asked sweetly.

"It was all right." His day had actually been stressful but he thought talking about it would only cause him to become stressed all over again. "I'm glad it's Friday!"

Mrs. Adler turned around and smiled sweetly at her husband, "Me, too!" He smiled back at his pretty wife.

"Are you hungry? Want a piece of garlic bread while we wait for the noodles to boil?"

Mr. Adler's stomach growled loudly right then and they both laughed.

"I'll take *that* as a 'yes!'," said Mrs. Adler as she took the buttery, crunchy, hot piece of bread out of the oven and placed it on her husband's plate in front of him. He immediately took a large bite and closed his eyes while he chewed. Mrs. Adler was a very good cook and Mr. Adler's waistline showed it. Mrs. Adler made pleasant small talk with her husband while she waited for him to finish the garlic bread.

Timing is everything in life! she told herself.

She took a deep breath then and tried to sound casual…

"Oh, um, Carli has a little surprise to show you in the TV room."

Mr. Adler raised his eyebrows at her. "Oh?"

"Let's go see," she said as she wiped her hands and started walking toward the TV room.

Mr. Adler was tired and didn't want to get up again so soon after getting home, but he was curious about the "surprise." When they walked into the TV room, Mr. Adler saw his daughter sitting next to her best friend, Molly. The kitten was so tiny that he didn't even notice her at first in his daughter's lap.

"Oh!," he said when he finally saw the kitten. "A kitten!?"

"Yeah, Daddy! Isn't she cute?!," said Carli excitedly. "Come and pet her." Carli patted the couch.

Mr. Adler walked over to Carli and knelt down next to the couch. He petted the tiny kitten's head and it squeaked at him three times.

"Kitten? Are you sure this is a kitten and not a *mouse*?!," teased Mr. Adler, frowning. "Maybe I need to get an *exterminator* in here!"

"Daddy!," reprimanded Carli, squinting her eyes and pointing at him.

Mr. Adler chuckled. He loved to tease his daughter.

"She's a cutey!," he said as he stroked the kitten's cheek. Squeaky began to purr.

Mrs. Adler smiled.

"Is she yours, Molly?," asked Mr Adler.

"No." Molly shook her head.

Mr. Adler looked up at his wife, lifted one eyebrow, and sighed. She cleared her throat nervously.

Wait for it thought Mr. Adler. And he didn't have to wait long...

"Can I *keep* her, Daddy?! She doesn't have a *home*! She lives underneath Molly's porch. Please, Daddy! Oh pleeeeeeeeeeeeease!" Carli's chin quivered as she looked pleadingly into her father's eyes.

The kitten purred loudly as Mr. Adler scratched behind her ear.

Gosh she's cute! he thought. He sighed heavily. He always had great difficulty saying "No" to his only child.

"Well,…if it's all right with your Mom, it's all right with me I guess."

Carli shivered with happiness but tried to keep her voice down to not scare the kitten. "Oh thank you, Daddy! Thank you! I love you sooo much!"

"Yeah, yeah," he said. "Let me see the baby." He took Squeaky from Carli and said, "Hello, cutie," while holding her close to his face. Squeaky promptly slapped him across the nose twice with her tiny nails out.

"Oh!," he chuckled. "Tough little thing, isn't she. Well, that'll be a nice change from Puff Puff." Mr. Adler frequently teased Carli about what a little scaredy-cat Puff Puff was.

"Daddy!," reprimanded Carli again, pouting at him. Mr. Adler laughed. He handed the kitten back to his daughter and stood up where he promptly received a grateful hug and kiss from his wife.

"What's one more little mouth to feed I guess, right?," he said cheerfully.

"Right!," replied Mrs. Adler. "Thank you, sweetheart." She affectionately brushed a bread crumb from his cheek.

Molly hoped that *her* father would feel the same way about taking in a kitten. She imagined her father *also* saying "*What's one more little mouth to feed?*" Molly smiled to herself at this thought.

"Oh! What if Puff Puff doesn't like the baby?," said Mrs. Adler.

Puff Puff rushed into the room just then looking for Squeaky. He saw her in Carli's lap and quickly ran to her. He jumped on the couch right next to his Carli and started licking Squeaky's tiny head. Squeaky closed her eyes and purred.

"I guess that answers *that* question!," said Mr. Adler, chuckling.

"Look! Puff Puff loves her!," said Carli gleefully.

"I'll make an appointment for her at the vet's," said Mrs. Adler. "No telling what kind of things she's contracted from living outside. Gotta get her in right away before she gives anything to Puff Puff. Now let's eat, everyone!"

We're keeping Squeaky! I'm a Dad! I'm a Dad! Puff Puff ran around the room three times excitedly and Molly and Carli laughed heartily together at him.

Molly's father came home late that night from work, tired and cranky. So Molly thought it would be better to wait and ask him about the kitten tomorrow on Saturday.

Chapter 11
It Takes a Village

The next morning, Molly cleaned the house and brought the newspaper inside to try to put her father in a good mood. Then she waited for him to come downstairs for breakfast. Mr. Taylor trudged down the stairs a little while later and made himself a cup of instant coffee.

"The house looks nice, Molly. Did you clean?"

"Yep."

"Thank you, sweetie! Go get my wallet."

Molly smiled. *Bubblegum money!* She scurried off to get her father's wallet from the table in the hall. Mr. Taylor opened his wallet, not knowing if there would be any money in it, but he saw two dollar bills there. He took them out and gave them to Molly for cleaning.

"Thank you, Daddy!" She quickly rolled up the bills and stuffed them into her pants pocket.

"Did you eat?," Mr. Taylor asked. "Do you want me to make you some eggs?" He brushed her scraggly hair out of her face affectionately.

"No, thank you. I ate toast and jelly." Mr. Taylor was not a good cook.

He had noticed the jelly on her cheeks and the big glob of jelly on her shirt but offered to make her breakfast in case she was still hungry.

"Where's Billy?," asked Mr. Taylor.

"He's still sleeping."

"Ah. The lazy bum!," said Mr. Taylor.

Molly giggled. She thought that her father seemed to be in a better mood than yesterday, so she crossed her fingers behind her back, took a deep breath, and said, "Daddy, can I please have a kitten?"

"No, honey, we can't afford it," Mr. Taylor answered immediately. "You already have Soupy. That's enough." He took a sip of coffee and opened up the newspaper.

Molly stood there quietly with her mouth hanging open. It felt like her whole world was crashing down around her. It had been so easy for Carli's father to agree to let Carli have a kitten. Why couldn't it work the same way for her!?

"But…," Molly said quietly. "But what's… what's one more little m'…mouth to feed?" Her lower lip trembled.

Mr. Taylor lowered the newspaper and looked at his little daughter and saw the destitution in her face. He immediately felt horrible. He put the paper down.

"Sweetie, we can't afford it. I'm sorry," he said sadly. His only charge card was up to its limit. He had to borrow the money for Billy and Molly's summer camp from his brother, Hal.

Molly abruptly ran out of the kitchen and out the front door. She couldn't *believe* that she had forgotten to be "tricky" like Marcy said and show her father the kitten when she asked him if she could keep him.

"Where are you going?!," called Mr. Taylor after her, frowning.

Molly reappeared a minute later cradling something in her hands. She walked up to her father and held tiny Hoppy up to his face.

"Where did you *get* that?!," said Mr. Taylor. He knew what Molly was trying to do.

"He lives under our porch with his momma. There were *two* kittens but Carli's dad let her keep the other kitten," explained Molly, with her chin quivering. She hoped hearing this would inspire her father to let her to keep this kitten.

Mr. Taylor closed his eyes and willed himself to be strong.

"I'm sorry, honey. We cannot afford a vet bill right now." His daughter's beautiful little face fell again. He felt like crying. He could see how badly she wanted to keep the kitten.

"Oh!" Molly held the kitten snugly with one hand and quickly dug into her pocket with the other hand for her two dollars. She held the bills up close to her father's face. "Here! You can have my two dollars back! And…and I have three more dollars upstairs!," she pleaded to her father desperately. She wished she hadn't bought all that bubble gum over the past few months. She would've had *eight* whole dollars to give to her father toward the vet bill if she hadn't.

"No, honey!" He closed his eyes again and shook his head. "Keep your money." He pushed her hand back toward her pocket. "It would cost much, much more than that for the spaying of the kitty and the shots. I'm sorry, honey. We simply *don't* have the money for another cat."

Molly's head dropped to her chest. A tear snuck out of her eye and rolled down her cheek. Mr. Taylor shook his head and buried his face in his hands. *Why is life always sooo hard?!*

He stood up. "I'm going to take a shower and then I'll take the kitten and its mother to the shelter for them to find good homes for them."

Molly gasped and looked up at her father in horror. She instinctively turned to the side protectively to put the kitten out of her traitorous father's reach. A sob escaped from Molly and tears now streamed freely down her little cheeks. Mr. Taylor quickly left the room before he broke into tears himself.

"I'LL TAKE THE KITTIES AND I'LL RUN AWAY FROM HOME!!," Molly screamed after her father. "I…I HATE YOUUUU!"

Mr. Taylor gasped. His little girl had never said this to him before. As he walked up the stairs, they blurred before him from the tears welling up in his eyes.

But where will we go?, thought Molly hopelessly. *I'm not even allowed to cross the street.*

She walked in a trance out the front door and back to the side of the porch. She quietly sat down in the grass next to the porch and placed the kitten inside the slats, sniffling. Hoppy scurried over to Beau and she licked his head. Beau sensed great sadness emanating from Molly and she had a strong urge to lick her head, too.

Molly was trying to be brave. All the cats gathered around her. They knew something was horribly wrong. Soupy climbed into her lap and licked her sticky face. Molly hugged Soupy tightly.

Molly loved Hoppy so much, it felt like her heart was breaking in half. She couldn't imagine her life without him. She couldn't believe that her father was going to take him away from her and bring him to the shelter along with the momma cat.

"I'll never know what happens to you now," Molly sniffled. "I'll never get to see you grow big." Two little rivers of tears ran down her face, drenching her shirt. "What if someone *mean* adopts you?" Molly buried her face in her hands.

Marcy walked up behind Molly with a big bowl of cat food and a fresh bowl of water. Even from behind, Marcy knew something was terribly wrong.

"What's wrong, Molly?! Are the kitties okay?!"

"Yes!" It came out as a sob.

Marcy sat down next to Molly and quickly put the food through the slats underneath the porch. Hoppy quickly hopped to the food and started eating. Marcy put her arm around Molly's shoulder.

"Did your dad say you couldn't keep the kitten?," asked Marcy softly.

Molly nodded her head slowly and then *burst* out crying at the top of her lungs! All the cats jumped back! Beau and Hoppy ran to the far corner under the porch!

"Oh, honey!" Marcy's eyes watered, too, now and she pulled Molly onto her lap and hugged her tightly. Her little body shook violently as she wailed uncontrollably into Marcy's shoulder, drenching her blouse with tears.

Cindy was in the backyard weeding and heard Molly burst out crying. "OH!" She threw down her weeder, quickly got up, and ran as fast as she could to Molly's house. She saw Marcy sitting in the grass next to the porch holding Molly while Molly wailed away at the top of her lungs.

Cindy hurried up to Marcy and put her hand on her shoulder. "What's wrong?! Did she fall off the porch?!"

"No. There's a Momma cat and a kitten living under her porch and her father told her she can't keep the kitten," Marcy spoke very loudly to be heard over Molly's sobbing. Molly wailed even louder when she heard Marcy say this because it made it all sound so final. Molly could barely catch her breath in between sobs.

Cindy sat on the ground next to Marcy and rubbed Molly's back. "Ooooh, poor Molly!"

"I HATE...MY...DADDYYYYYYY!," sobbed Molly.

"Oh, no you don't, honey," said Marcy. "He simply doesn't have the money. He loves you very much and if he could afford to give you another kitten, I'm *sure* he would."

Molly listened to Marcy but it didn't help and she continued to sob uncontrollably.

Cindy peered underneath the porch to get a look at the cat and kitten and she saw Beau.

"Oh! I've seen that cat before! Out in the field with Lila a few days ago. I didn't know she had a kitten!" Cindy spoke loudly close to Marcy's ear so she could hear her over Molly's wailing.

"There were *two* kittens, but Carli took one," explained Marcy.

This caused Molly to wail even louder at the unfairness of it all! Marcy thought it sounded like someone was torturing the poor child! Marcy couldn't bear hearing her little Molly's sobs any longer. It was breaking her heart. Marcy made a decision!

"You can *KEEP* the kitten, Molly!," proclaimed Marcy loudly into Molly's ear. "At *my* house!"

Molly's sobs finally slowed a little. She choked and gasped for air.

Marcy said, "It will be YOUR kitten. It will just live at *my* house. Okay?"

Molly sniffled and wiped her running nose on the back of her sleeve. She wiped her eyes with her hands and looked up into Marcy's face.

"Re…really?," she stuttered, breathing hard.

Cindy smiled at Marcy. "Awww. You are *so* sweet!"

Marcy smiled back at Cindy. "Well, you know what they say...'It takes a village to raise a child!'"

Now that Molly had stopped crying and was just sniffling and hiccupping, Marcy put her on the ground next to Cindy.

Molly was trying to catch her breath. She wanted to make sure that she understood. "Y'... you mean you'll keep the kitt .. kitten at your house, but it will really be *m'* .. *my* kitten?" She blinked several times nervously.

"Yes!," proclaimed Marcy. "It will absolutely be *your* kitten but it will just live at *my* house. You can pick the name of the kitty because he's yours, and you can come visit him whenever you want, A HUNDRED times a day if you want!" Marcy threw her arms in the air dramatically when she said "A HUNDRED."

Molly finally smiled. Then she giggled nervously. She was scared to believe it. She sniffled and wiped her eyes again.

"And you can feed him and you can come with me to the vet's with him and everything."

Now Molly couldn't stop smiling. She had her kitten! A few seconds ago, it felt like her whole world had come to an end. But now, thanks to her Marcy, everything was all right again.

Molly suddenly lurched forward and hugged Marcy tightly. "I love you!" She closed her eyes tightly and the last two tears in her eyes squeezed out and ran down her cheeks.

"I love you, too, honey." Marcy closed her eyes, too, and enjoyed her hug.

"Oh!," exclaimed Molly as she suddenly pushed away from Marcy! She clumsily dug into her pocket, and Marcy wondered what she was looking for. Molly pulled out her two crumpled dollar bills and held them up to Marcy's face.

"I can help pay for the vet bills! And...and I have three more dollars in my room from doing my chores, so I can give you that, too." Molly pointed up toward her bedroom and smiled proudly at Marcy.

Marcy's first instinct was to tell Molly to keep her money, but then she thought if she accepted the money, it might help Molly's feeling that the kitten truly was hers.

"Well, okay! Thank you!" Marcy took the bills from Molly and held them up, smiling.

Molly clasped her hands together and laughed. "Welcome!" Molly looked so proud then that Marcy knew she made the right decision to accept her money.

Molly wiped her nose again on her sleeve and said, "N'…now all we have to do is find a home for the momma cat." She gestured toward Beau under the porch.

"Oh no we don't!," proclaimed Cindy jubilantly, shaking her head back and forth. "I already found the Momma cat a home…" Cindy pointed at herself with both her thumbs and smiled from ear to ear. "MINE!"

"OH!," exclaimed Marcy and Molly in unison.

"You?! You're going to keep the Momma cat?," asked Marcy excitedly.

"I sure am!" Cindy laughed. "So now…*everyone* has a home!" Cindy outstretched both arms and looked up at the sky dramatically.

Molly and Marcy laughed together at Cindy's theatrics. Molly lurched at Cindy and gave her a grateful hug, too. Cindy hugged Molly tightly.

"This is wonderful! Now we don't have to separate their little family. I'm going to go call the vet and get *your* new kitten in for an appointment," said Marcy, poking Molly softly in the nose. Molly sniffled and laughed bashfully.

"Me, too!," said Cindy as she got up from the ground.

"I'm gonna go tell Daddy that we don't have to take the kitties to the shelter!," said Molly joyfully as she got up and ran inside the house.

❋ ❋ ❋

With the help of Molly, Cindy tricked Beau and got her into a cat carrier and brought her to the vet's office. Cindy had left a large cat carrier by Molly's porch every day for several days until Beau took no notice of it any more. Then one day, Cindy brought liver sausage, Beau's favorite treat, to her in a bowl and placed it next to the opening of the carrier. While Beau was entranced with eating her liver sausage, Cindy grabbed Beau under her two front legs and quickly thrust her in the carrier while Molly closed the carrier door behind her.

"What a team we are!," said Cindy to Molly. Molly laughed and clapped her hands together, celebrating their covert mission of tricking little Beau into the carrier.

Cindy promptly stood up and drove Beau to the vet's office for her appointment.

"No more kittens for *you*, little missy!," said Cindy to Beau on the way there.

Beau was spayed and vaccinated, and her fleas, ear mites, and worms were all taken care of. After recovering from her surgery, Beau couldn't believe how wonderful she felt without having to scratch fleas and ear mites all the time.

The vet told Cindy, though, that they would not do anything about Beau's crooked leg because it obviously didn't hurt her any longer, and resetting the leg would be painful and dangerous for Beau. And so it was that Beau's little crooked leg would remain crooked. But Cindy and Steve actually enjoyed having a little crooked-legged cat because, as Cindy always said, "Variety is the spice of life!"

Chapter 12
Shmoopy, Bopey, and Mopey to the Rescue!

A couple of weeks passed and little Squeaky and Hoppy had adjusted to life as indoor pets very well. They were quite enjoying being able to sleep in a soft bed every night and have fresh bowls of food and water whenever they were hungry or thirsty. And the best part was that they still were able to see their Momma every day. Hoppy was happy because now he could hop on Spider Man's stomach whenever he wanted. Beau was extremely relieved and happy that both her kittens lived right next door to her so she could see them every day.

One morning very early, when the sun had just peeked over the horizon, little Squeaky woke up. She had fallen asleep very early the night before and was now refreshed and ready for a new day even though Carli and Puff Puff were still sleeping deeply next to her. Squeaky wanted someone to play with, so she walked over to Puff Puff and squeaked loudly two times right into his ear. This didn't wake him, so she poked him in the face two times. That didn't wake him either but it did cause him to cover his face with both paws. Squeaky jumped on Puff Puff's shoulder now and bit him in the head but he just gently pushed her away and kept sleeping. Squeaky pouted at her father.

So she walked over to Carli's head and squeaked loudly right into her ear, too. Carli did not stir, so Squeaky picked up a lock of Carli's hair in her mouth and yanked it back and forth with all her might. But Carli slept on. Squeaky spit out the lock of hair and glared at Carli. She walked up close to Carli and smacked her in the head as hard as she could two times. Squeaky giggled at the funny "Whap! Whap!" noise it made when she smacked Carli. So she smacked her in the head another two times just to hear the "Whap! Whap!" noise again. She giggled even harder this time. But again, there was no reaction from the deeply sleeping little Carli. Squeaky was very frustrated now. She climbed onto Carli's face and plopped her little furry body down right across Carli's nose and mouth. Carli simply turned over, causing Squeaky to roll onto the pillow. Squeaky stood up and stomped on the pillow angrily.

She finally gave up on waking Puff Puff or Carli and jumped off the bed and went downstairs. She went into the kitchen and drank from her water bowl and crunched on a little hard cat food. Squeaky was afraid to go outside without Puff Puff but out of curiosity, she walked to the cat door and peeked out onto the back yard. It was very quiet and peaceful. She looked around nervously.

I wish Daddah would wake up! I want someone to pway wiff. (Translation: I want someone to play with.)

A small white butterfly flew by the cat door. Without a thought, Squeaky dashed out the cat door and ran after it! She caught up to the butterfly and batted it with a tiny paw. The butterfly flew off course for a second and, sensing danger, flew higher away from the creature who just batted her. Squeaky chased the butterfly through Carli's backyard out onto the open field behind it.

❈ ❈ ❈

The sun had just risen and the large raptor woke up very hungry. He left the forest preserve and flew high in the sky in search of a tasty squirrel or rabbit. Off in the distance across the long field, the hawk's sharp vision caught some movement. He turned and recognized the creature. His eyes widened.

I remember you, he smiled evilly. The little animal was all alone this time. *No fluffy white friend to protect you now, hmm?*

The hawk turned and flew toward Squeaky.

✳ ✳ ✳

Most cats are extremely perceptive and can actually sense danger approaching. They can also feel silent emotions from others around them. *Imaginary* cats are even more perceptive than real cats.

Shmoopy, Bopey, and Mopey woke up very early that morning, too. Well, Mopey *tried* to sleep in, but Shmoopy and Bopey pulled on her tail and ears until she got up to play with them. The three colorful cats chased each other up and down trees, batting each other in the head playfully and laughing.

Mopey dashed up a very tall pine tree and Shmoopy chased after her, laughing. After Mopey climbed very high, over 60 feet in the air, she whirled around and slapped Shmoopy right in the face!

"OUCH!" Shmoopy held her cheek and bared her teeth at Mopey. "Grrrrrr!" Shmoopy took her fist and bonked Mopey on the top of her head and then laughed heartily at the hollow "thump" sound that Mopey's head made.

Mopey grasped her head with both paws. She curled her lips back and hissed at Shmoopy.

"Uh oh!," said Shmoopy. Mopey looked furious!

She quickly turned and ran from Mopey to the end of the branch. The thinning branch bent drastically and almost broke under her weight.

"Oh no!," Shmoopy gasped! She quickly clutched the branch tightly with her nails and looked back at Mopey fearfully.

Mopey saw her chance for revenge and quickly climbed over to Shmoopy on a thicker branch directly above her. Shmoopy was now dangling dangerously from the thinning branch by her two front paws. Her body slowly swung back and forth high up in the tree. Shmoopy looked down to the ground so far below her and became dizzy. Mopey reached out and plucked three of Shmoopy's fingers off the branch.

"Mopey, stop it!," yelled Shmoopy, gaping at her. She slid down the branch a little further. "I'm gonna fall!,"

Mopey smiled wickedly and plucked three more fingers off the branch. "*That* will teach you to bonk *me* on the head!"

"Mopey! We're so high! Please stop!," Shmoopy begged for her life.

Mopey snickered and mercilessly plucked Shmoopy's last two fingers off the branch. Shmoopy shrieked in horror and began her long descent to the ground. Mopey gleefully watched as her sister fell, trying to grasp the other branches on her way down. At first, it seemed like Shmoopy was falling in slow motion. But the farther she fell, the faster she went. Mopey stopped smiling and her expression slowly changed to dread as she watched Shmoopy fall closer and closer to the ground, screaming the whole way. When Mopey had plucked Shmoopy's last two fingers off the branch, she was *sure* that Shmoopy would be able to catch another branch on her way down to stop her fall. They played this game all the time and Shmoopy was *always* able to grab another branch.

But this time, all of Shmoopy's attempts to stop her fall failed, and she finally landed on the ground with a ghastly, final thud, which echoed throughout the forest over and over and over again. Bopey and Mopey gasped in horror!

Shmoopy laid there on the floor of the forest, perfectly still and quiet.

Bopey and Mopey quickly climbed down their trees and gathered around Shmoopy's body lying face down and motionless in the leaves.

They took hold of each other's paws for strength and gaped at their sister's lifeless body.

"Oh no," whispered Bopey, shaking her head slowly back and forth.

Mopey closed her eyes and hung her head in shame and grief. The entire forest was perfectly silent in reverence for their poor Shmoopy. Every bird had stopped chirping. The wind ceased blowing. Even the creek's current came to a complete halt.

"What did I do…?," whispered Mopey mournfully.

Now an interesting fact about *imaginary* cats is that they are quite durable. What might easily *kill* a *real* cat will merely slow an imaginary cat down but for a moment.

Shmoopy slowly lifted her face off the ground and looked around the forest with crossed eyes.

"What…happened?," she asked dazedly. Leaves and twigs stuck to her face, and two small twigs stuck to her lips.

When Bopey and Mopey saw this, they pointed at Shmoopy's face and burst out laughing so hard that they fell on the ground.

Shmoopy shook the twigs and leaves from her face and spit the twigs from her lips. This caused Bopey and Mopey to laugh even harder. Bopey held her sides and Mopey pounded the ground, still pointing at Shmoopy. They rocked back and forth on the ground shrieking with laughter together.

Shmoopy turned and glowered at Mopey with her eyes still crossed. She stood up slowly and brushed the leaves off the rest of her body, staggering back and forth.

Mopey and Bopey stifled their laughter now, but they held their paws to their mouths trying to hide the giggling that they just couldn't stop.

Shmoopy's lips curled back and an ominous low growl emitted from deep inside her chest. "Just wait'll I get my paws on you!" She pointed at Mopey.

"Uh oh!," said Mopey, wide-eyed.

Mopey scrambled to her feet and dashed to the nearest tree and Shmoopy ran after her. Mopey started climbing up the tree, but Shmoopy caught up to her and grabbed the big ball of fur at the end of her tail. Shmoopy held tight to the end of Mopey's tail, but instead of stopping Mopey, she continued up the tree, and Shmoopy was left standing on the ground looking at a big ball of green fur in her paw with a dumbfounded expression on her face. Mopey stopped a few feet above Shmoopy, pointed at her, and guffawed loudly. She stuck out her tongue and blew raspberries at Shmoopy. With a popping sound, another long ball of fur instantly grew back at the end of Mopey's tail.

"Nya nya nya nya nya nya!," taunted Mopey as she wiggled her new ball of fur right in Shmoopy's face.

"Ooooh!," said Shmoopy, baring her teeth. She hurled the green ball of fur on the ground and furiously stomped on it several times, hissing and spitting! This made Mopey guffaw even louder and pound on the tree with her paw.

Shmoopy turned to the tree and dug her front claws into it, preparing to chase after Mopey and tear her to shreds, but she abruptly froze in place as a horrible chill ran up her spine and she shivered. She turned toward the houses, placed a paw over her heart, and drew in her breath in horror!

Mopey dashed down the tree, grabbed Shmoopy's shoulders and looked into her eyes.

"What's *wrong*?!," Mopey gaped at Shmoopy.

"We have to go!"

Mopey turned and looked across the field toward the houses, too, now. "The killer bird is *BACK*!"

Bopey had joined her sisters again and said, "It's gonna eat SQUEAKY!" Her purple fur stood on end.

Without another word, they turned and tore across the field toward the houses.

"But what can *we* do?! We're only *imaginary* cats!," screamed Mopey with a look of horror on her face as she ran.

They knew Squeaky was mere seconds away from *death*.

"*Beau* could see us!," screamed Shmoopy as the three raced across the long field with unimaginable speed. "Maybe the *monster bird* will be able to see us, too!"

"We have to *try* to *save* her!," screamed Bopey, breathing hard.

The raptor was diving now, soaring through the air toward the tiny animal. Squeaky was completely unaware that she was going to be a hawk's breakfast in a matter of seconds. She merrily jumped at the little butterfly who seemed to be teasing her now, coming close and then flying high again when Squeaky was about to catch her.

The hungry raptor glared at the little animal and he began to salivate.

Shmoopy, Bopey, and Mopey didn't know this, but Beau's great love for them had made their existence just a little stronger in the real world.

The hawk noticed something out of the corner of his eye and quickly turned his head toward the forest. A colorful hazy cloud was racing across the field directly toward the tiny creature. The cloud was blue, purple, and green and moving with incredible speed! He quickly opened his wings and slowed down his flight. When the colorful cloud reached the baby, it abruptly stopped and surrounded it. Squeaky stopped chasing the butterfly because she saw that she was surrounded by a beautiful cloud. She felt the warmth of Shmoopy, Bopey, and Mopey's bodies around her. Squeaky stood still now and marveled at the beautiful, warm cloud. She lifted her arm and curiously passed it through the cloud.

How odd, thought the hawk. He had never seen a cloud those colors before or one that could control its own movement like that. He turned and quickly flew higher in the sky, considering the strange cloud carefully.

"He's LEAVING!," yelled Bopey, breathlessly.

"Oh thank *goodness*!," said Mopey, wiping her forehead. "Thank *goodness*!"

"We DID it!," exclaimed Shmoopy, her chest heaving. "I can't *believe* it!"

The girls looked at each other and laughed heartily together in celebration of their successful mission of saving tiny Squeaky. Their breath started to return to normal.

Up in the sky, the large raptor was watching the colorful cloud warily.

Can a cloud hurt me? he asked himself, slowly circling the sky again. *I've flown threw clouds many times.* His stomach growled in hunger and he sneered resentfully. *I want that baby for breakfast!* He turned and began another descent toward the animal.

"NOOOO!" Mopey pointed up at the sky. "IT'S COMING BACK!"

"NOOOOO!," screamed Shmoopy and Bopey together.

All three imaginary cats shook violently in terror. They stood with their arms around their friend's baby gaping up at the killer bird soaring directly at her again. Mopey made a decision!

"I'M GOING TO BITE IT!," she screamed.

"YES! BITE IT WITH YOUR TIGER FANGS!," Shmoopy and Bopey screamed in unison.

Mopey quickly placed her body directly in front of Squeaky. She curled her lips back and opened her mouth as wide as she could. All three girls imagined Mopey's long fangs sinking into the raptor's body.

While soaring toward the tiny creature again, the hawk saw the colorful cloud shift. The green section of the cloud clearly repositioned itself directly in front of the animal.

Mopey concentrated with all her might and imagined her sharp incisors piercing the monster's flesh. She would bite down as hard as she could and hold on as long as possible.

What is that?! The hawk squinted at the cloud.

Two hazy, very long sharp *FANGS* appeared within the front green section of the cloud!

The hawk's eyes widened and he let out an ear-splitting screech! He whipped open his wings as wide as possible to stop in mid-flight, but he lost control and did three summersaults in the air. Feathers swirled all around him. He regained control a few feet above the evil fanged cloud and quickly made a hard right turn. He soared back to the forest preserve screeching in terror the whole way. He looked back over his shoulder several times to make sure the fanged cloud was not coming after him.

✳ ✳ ✳

Beau and Puff Puff were still sleeping, but the hawk's piercing screeches woke them. They jumped up immediately, scared to the bone, knowing instinctively that Squeaky was in terrible danger. Puff Puff feared he was already too late.

Beau dashed through Cindy's back yard toward the field, chanting *"MY BABY! MY BABY! MY BABY!"*

Puff Puff jumped off Carli's bed and tore down the stairs as fast as he could. His claws made scratching noises on the carpet. He darted out the cat door toward the field.

Beau and Puff Puff saw Squeaky in the field at the same time. The raptor's screeching had terrified her and she was laying flat on the ground covering her eyes with both paws and trembling. Puff Puff noticed that she seemed to be surrounded by a vibrantly colored haze and wondered about this. They saw the large hawk in the distance soaring toward the forest preserve as fast as it could, still screeching in panic, glancing back over his shoulder again and again. Puff Puff wondered if the hawk was afraid of the colorful cloud for some reason.

Beau reached Squeaky first and quickly licked her head and face. Squeaky clutched her mother's leg. The beautiful cloud moved away from Squeaky now and floated in place a few feet away, shimmering beautifully in the early morning light.

"Thank you! Oh, thank you!," said Beau emotionally, her chin quivering.

Puff Puff thought it seemed as though Beau was talking to the cloud. The colorful cloud floated back and surrounded both Beau and Squeaky for a moment as Shmoopy, Bopey, and Mopey hugged them. Beau closed her eyes and smiled when the cloud did this. Then the beautiful cloud slowly floated off toward the forest on a warm breeze.

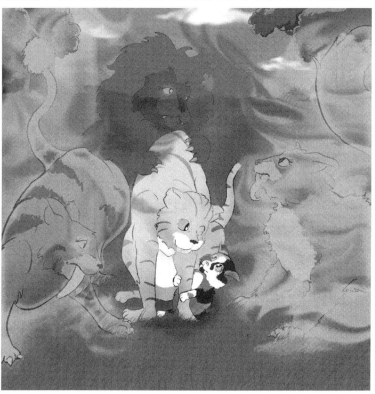

Beau grabbed Squeaky by the scruff of the neck and ran toward the porch with Puff Puff at her heals.

"What ah you doin', Momma?! Put me down!," complained Squeaky with a pouty face. "I wanna catch d' bubbafye!" (Translation: "I want to catch the butterfly!") She pointed back toward the field as she was being carried.

Beau ignored Squeaky's complaints and kept running as fast as she could with a chubby kitten in her mouth. When they reached the porch, Beau clumsily placed Squeaky through the slats and then climbed through herself. Puff Puff followed. Beau and Puff Puff stood there panting for a minute. Squeaky jumped on Puff Puff's back and bit his shoulder.

"It's about time you gotted up, you wazy poo-poo-head!," said Squeaky to her father. (Translation: It's about time you gotted up, you lazy poo-poo-head!)

Puff Puff and Beau looked at each other and laughed. Squeaky laughed, too, then.

"I had no one to pway wiff,!" Squeaky pouted.

When Beau's breathing returned to normal, she said sternly, "Squeaky!"

Squeaky stood at attention. From her mother's tone of voice, she knew she was in big trouble. She looked down at the ground not quite sure what she had done wrong.

"You do NOT go outside all alone! You're too little and it's dangerous!," lectured Beau, frowning at her tiny daughter.

Squeaky just blinked. She had no idea that she had almost been a predator's breakfast.

"Promise us!," said Puff Puff, pointing at her.

"I pwomise!," Squeaky said obediently, nodding just once. But she pouted. She did not like being scolded.

Beau and Puff Puff were quiet for a moment.

"All right. Good girl," said Beau. She licked Squeaky's face. Squeaky grabbed her mother's head and bit her cheek.

❈ ❈ ❈

After scaring the hawk away, Shmoopy, Bopey, and Mopey walked back to the forest breathing heavily.

"The killer bird could *see* us!," said Shmoopy in wonder, smiling.

"He sure could!," declared Bopey proudly.

"Well, thank goodness he could see Mopey's big *fangs*!," said Shmoopy, touching the sharp tip of one of Mopey's long incisors. "*That's* the most important thing!"

"See?!," said Mopey. She stopped walking and pointed at her Bopey and Shmoopy. "I *told* you they would come in handy some day!"

"You *did*!," said Bopey, patting Mopey's back.

"That sure was scary!," said Mopey, blinking quickly and looking up at the sky.

"I've never been so ascared in my *life*!," said Shmoopy, wringing her front paws together.

"Let's go get some breakfast. I'm hungry," said Bopey.

"Me, too," said Mopey. "I'm gonna eat that rainbow over there." She pointed to a beautiful little rainbow that had formed over the creek in the morning mist.

"I'm gonna eat those clouds over there." Shmoopy pointed to two little clouds hanging low in the sky over the forest.

"Hmmm. I think I'm gonna eat the sun," said Bopey. She squinted up at the sun.

"You can't eat the *sun*, Silly-Pants!," said Shmoopy, giggling.

"Why *not*?!" Bopey pointed at Shmoopy and sneered. "*You're* not the *boss* of *me*!"

"Well," Shmoopy gestured all around. "'Cause it would be too *dark* outside during the day without any sun!"

Mopey pointed at a patch of beautiful wild flowers growing at the edge of the forest. "And the flowers wouldn't grow, Bopey!" She knew Bopey loved flowers.

Bopey looked at the beautiful flowers and thought about this for a second. "Oh. Yeah, you're right."

"You can have half my rainbow," offered Mopey.

Bopey smiled. "Thanks!"

All three girls had the same thought as they ate their delicious breakfast together...*It was nice to be seen by someone else besides Beau for a change!*

Chapter 13
The Pine Cone Gift

Soupy had run to the forest preserve about three times a week all summer long and continued into fall in search of his Ferdinand. But he had not been able to find him, and he was slowly giving up hope. The other cats had stopped accompanying Soupy on his trips because they couldn't bear to look at his disappointed little face any longer. Soupy hated to think about what might have happened to his beloved son. It was dangerous out there in the world with dogs, and fast cars, and killer birds in the sky. After dinner one day, Billy ran outside to play and carelessly left the front door open. So Soupy thought he would give it another try to find Ferdinand.

It was 6:00 p.m. and it was getting dark because it was late October now. But that didn't matter to Soupy because cats can see fairly well in the dark. Soupy had never searched the forest in the dark before. He ran the three blocks to the forest in about two minutes. There were leaves on the ground now and they crackled under his feet as he ran.

When he reached the forest, as usual he ran all around the border and then through the inner forest, calling "FERDINAAAAAND!" over and over again. But no one answered. He stood at the edge of the forest for a moment.

*Where **are** you, my son?*

He laid down in the grass to rest for a minute. He stared into the forest hopelessly, but slowly noticed something familiar off to his left. It was the hollow log where he had lived and raised Ferdinand. He stood up and walked inside the log and found that it still smelled of Ferdinand. He inhaled deeply and sat there for a moment remembering his son when he was a baby. He was so tiny when he first found Ferdinand that Soupy could carry him around by the scruff of his neck. He remembered Ferdinand scurrying after him wherever they went. He remembered how Ferdinand would run to him for a comforting hug when something scared him even when he grew bigger. Soupy remembered how they filled their days laughing and playing hide and seek and chasing each other up and down trees.

He breathed a heavy sigh. His heart felt like it weighed a thousand pounds.

*Maybe…*Soupy slowly shook his head back and forth…*maybe my memories will be **all** that I have left of my boy.*

He hung his head and a teardrop spilled out of his eye onto the ground. He wiped his face with the back of his paw and sniffled. A second teardrop fell out of his other eye.

It was very dark now, so Soupy left the hollow log, his old tiny home, and turned toward the houses. But he stopped. He felt a little silly, but he thought…

*Just one more try. Just **one** more…*He faced the forest again and took a deep breath…

"FERDINAAAAAAAND!," he called as loudly as he could. He stared into the forest and waited, not really expecting anything to happen.

But he heard *something*. He cocked his head. It was coming from within the forest. Leaves crackling. Soupy backed up.

The crackling was getting louder and faster. Soupy saw two eyes glowing in the dark coming at him from the forest. He was about to make a run for it but as the eyes came closer, he saw that a masked face framed them. It was a huge raccoon running toward him as fast as it could, making excited chittering noises.

"OH!," exclaimed Soupy. He knew that voice anywhere! "IT'S FERDINAND! IT'S MY FERDINAND!!" His heart soared a thousand feet high!

Soupy dashed to his son and reached him in an instant. "OH FERDINAND!"

Ferdinand grabbed his father and hugged him tightly. They fell in the leaves on the ground together and Ferdinand buried his head into Soupy's chest like he used to when he was little. Soupy laid his face on Ferdinand's head and breathed him in. He loved the way his son smelled. He licked Ferdinand's head over and over again. Ferdinand closed his eyes and held Soupy like he never wanted to let him go.

"Oh Ferdinand, I thought I'd never find you!" He licked Ferdinand's ears and Ferdinand chattered gleefully.

Soupy felt someone watching them and he looked up to see Ruthie at the edge of the forest.

"Oh, hi, Ruthie!," said Soupy, smiling broadly at her.

Ruthie warbled jovially at Ferdinand's funny-looking little orange father.

Soupy and Ferdinand visited for a half an hour, chasing each other and wrestling while Ruthie watched and laughed at them. But then Soupy thought that he better be getting home for the night. He didn't want Molly to worry about him.

"I have to go, son," said Soupy. He looked in the direction of home.

Ferdinand seemed to understand but he looked worried. He stood still and looked deep into Soupy's eyes, wringing his hands together nervously.

"I'll be back, Ferdinand. I promise!," said Soupy. "I'll visit you every chance I get!" He nodded enthusiastically.

Again Ferdinand seemed to understand and chattered at Soupy, nodding his head. Soupy started walking toward home. Ferdinand suddenly chortled loudly at him, so Soupy stopped and looked at Ferdinand again. Ferdinand dashed back into the forest. A few seconds later, he was running toward Soupy again. Soupy smiled. When he reached Soupy, Ferdinand dropped a pine cone at his feet.

"Oh! A present!," said Soupy. "Thank you, son!"

Ferdinand plopped on the ground on his back, held onto his feet, and rocked back and forth excitedly. Then he scrambled up and scurried over to Ruthie. He turned around and looked back at Soupy from the edge of the forest with Ruthie.

"By, Son. By, Ruthie." Soupy waved.

They both chattered back at him and nodded. Soupy picked up his pine cone in his mouth and ran home.

When he got home, Soupy put his pine cone in the middle of Molly's pillow for safekeeping. When Molly went to her room later that night to go to bed, she noticed the pine cone on her pillow. She picked it up, turned it over to examine it, and wondered where it came from. She walked over and threw the pine cone in her little wastebasket in the corner of her room. Quite offended, Soupy dashed over to the wastebasket and tipped it on its side with his paw.

"Oh! What are you doing, silly goose?," asked Molly giggling.

Soupy dug through the bubblegum wrappers that had spilled out onto the carpet and found his present from his son. He picked it up in his mouth, scurried back to Molly's bed, and jumped up on it. He walked up to her pillow and carefully placed the pine cone back upon it. He turned and looked accusingly at Molly.

"Oh, is this a *special* pine cone?," she asked while scratching his chin. Soupy purred.

"Okay, then I won't *ever* throw it away again. I promise." She nodded just once. And she never did.

Soupy couldn't wait until tomorrow when he saw all his friends to tell them that he had finally found his son. It was Lila who figured out then that maybe the trick to finding Ferdinand was to wait until after dusk because raccoons might sleep during the day.

When it wasn't horribly cold that winter, Soupy visited Ferdinand a couple of times a week. In the spring, Soupy got to meet his tiny grandchildren when Ruthie gave birth to a baby girl and a baby boy. Ferdinand and Ruthie named the baby boy "Soupy" in his honor. They named their baby girl ZoomZoom because she was an impressively fast runner for such a little raccoon.

✷ ✷ ✷

So life went on for the neighborhood. Puff Puff and Squeaky lived happily ever after with Carli.

It took months for Beau to trust Cindy and Steve enough to move into their house with them. Every day, Cindy moved Beau's food and water bowls closer to their cat door to get Beau used to eating in their kitchen. When it started to get very cold outside in late fall was when Beau finally started sleeping inside the house instead of underneath the porch. It took six months for Beau to be able to trust Cindy and Steve enough to allow them to pet her but once she did, her purring was so loud that they named her "Purrty."

Beau and her beloved imaginary friends, Shmoopy, Bopey, and Mopey, visited each other regularly. Beau lived to the ripe old age of 22 but never forgot how they bravely saved her baby from the hawk that one very early morning.

Molly's father was incredibly thankful to Marcy for taking in little Hoppy for Molly, although he was too embarrassed to tell Marcy how grateful he was. But to show his gratitude and to reinforce Molly's feeling that she was Hoppy's owner, every couple of months if Mr. Taylor had a little money, he would buy extra cat food for Molly to give to Marcy for Hoppy. This always made Molly proud that she was doing her part as Hoppy's *true* owner.

Cindy and Steve, of course, showered their three furry daughters with love and affection for the rest of their lives.

Soupy, Spider Man, and Hoppy were quite spoiled by Marcy and Molly for the rest of their lives, as all animals should be.

The great heroines, Shmoopy, Bopey, and Mopey, lived happily ever after in the beautiful forest preserve together.

And our beautiful, sweet Beau would never ever be cold, hungry, or lonely again.

Epilogue

Princess' owner, Lucci, loved Princess very much but she worked long hours every week, so Princess was feeling lonely again. For a while, she had enjoyed having company whenever Beau came to visit, but months had gone by now without another visit. So Princess assumed that Beau had finally found a home. The summer before, Princess had greatly enjoyed when Soupy and Ferdinand had visited her but they eventually stopped visiting also. Princess assumed that Soupy had finally found his way home to his little ragamuffin owner, Molly. And Ferdinand, Soupy's raccoon-foster-kitten, never really talked to Princess, so she didn't mind that he stopped visiting her anyway. Besides, the fact was that Princess thought herself *much* too good to be seen with a lowly dumb, wild raccoon.

But then she thought, *Well, Soupy could still come back and visit if he* really *wanted because Molly told Lucci that they only lived three blocks away. A cat can run three blocks in two minutes!"* Princess pouted.

Princess thought of how she used to make fun of Beau for her scraggly appearance. Princess wondered if maybe that was why Beau stopped visiting.

Princess remembered Beau's crooked leg, her chipped fang, and her bloodied ears from her ear mites. She could still see in her mind the sunken hole on Beau's sad face where her left eye used to be. Princess thought then that it must be hard to live outside with no owner. Princess began to feel a little bad for teasing Beau all the time.

Then Princess remembered how she had teased Ferdinand, too, when he wasn't feeling well by chanting "Ferdinand Fart-Pants! Ferdinand Fart-Pants!" at him. She remembered how angry Soupy had been at her for teasing his son. It occurred to Princess then that maybe the reason she had no friends was because she just wasn't a very nice cat. This made Princess feel bad about herself. She wished she could go back in time and have another chance with Soupy and Beau. If she could have another chance, she would be extra specially nice to them so that they would keep visiting her forever. Princess smiled at this thought.

She laid down under her favorite peony bush all alone and felt sorry for herself. She also experienced another emotion that she had never felt before…*shame*. And she didn't like being ashamed of herself, not one bit.

That night, while in the backyard, Princess looked up at the sky and she saw a large bright wishing star. Princess didn't really believe in wishing stars, but she thought *It couldn't hurt to make a wish, could it?* Before she began, she thought carefully about the best way to talk to a wishing star. She took a deep breath.

"Oh please, big, beautiful, shiny Wishing Star…" Princess thought *Flattery never hurts*. "…Please make Soupy and Beau come back to visit me again. If you do, I promise, promise, *promise* that I'll be very nice to them this time so that they'll wanna be my friends forever and *ever!*" Princess smiled, picturing Beau and Soupy in her backyard again.

The brightly shining Wishing Star saw the beautiful blue-eyed cat looking up at him and he heard her wish and her flattery. And the Star was, in fact, quite flattered. The cat seemed truly sincere and she looked so sad. The Star sensed her unbearable loneliness.

"Hmmm," said the Wishing Star. "I think I'll grant the rotten little *bully* one more chance!" Suddenly, the star brightened, doubled in size, and surged right toward Princess! She jumped back, lost her footing, and did three backward summer-saults into her peony bush!

She cowered inside the shrub for a moment, but her curiosity got the best of her and she cautiously crawled out of the shrub. Princess peered up at the beautiful Wishing Star to see if something else would happen. She waited to feel something or hear something, perhaps Soupy or Beau crawling underneath the fence into the yard. But a while passed and nothing else happened, so Princess wondered if she had imagined the sudden brightness of the star. She yawned, walked through her cat door, and then climbed up the stairs to the second floor. Princess trudged into Lucci's bedroom, jumped up on the bed, snuggled close to Lucci, and fell asleep.

Her last sad thought was *I'm NEVER gonna have any friends again!* She fell asleep with a little pouty expression on her face.

But the forgiving Wishing Star wanted to see if the mean little bully could change her ways and finally be nice to someone, nice enough to keep a friend…or maybe even…*eight* friends! The Wishing Star wasn't going to make it easy for this spoiled, rude cat. He snickered to himself because he was going to present Princess with a real *challenge*. He was going to send her eight very "different" possible friends. And if Princess wasn't kind to *them*, he would never *ever* grant her another wish!

The very next morning, Lucci left for work very early. It was actually still a little dark outside, so there were still some stars shining dimly in the sky. Princess trudged into the back yard and laid down under the peony bush ready for another long lonely day. A moment later, though, she heard someone coming.

"Oh!," she gasped! "Beau!? Soupy?!" Princess couldn't believe that the kind Wishing Star had granted her wish and so quickly! She jumped up and dashed out from underneath the peony and looked around the back yard.

"What...?!," said Princess as she stopped abruptly.

She was face to face with a very strange-looking creature. The creature had seven smaller versions of herself, all riding on her back, holding tightly to her coarse-looking grey fur. All of them looked at Princess warily. The Momma opened her mouth to show Princess her many, many teeth as a warning not to try to hurt any of her babies.

Princess stared back at the Momma and she couldn't believe how many teeth she had. She looked at the creature's strange bald tail and frowned. Princess also noticed that she had big cute mouse ears and cute little bald, pink fingers. But instead of focusing on the creature's cute ears and fingers, she prepared to tease her about having so many teeth and an ugly tail. Princess snickered rudely and opened her mouth to deliver her insults, but something twinkled very brightly in the sky for a couple of seconds right then. She gaped up at the sky and her mouth snapped shut!

"Oh!," she said as she covered her mouth with her paw. "I almost forgot!"

The Momma looked up at the sky where Princess had looked but she saw nothing unusual. She squinted her eyes at Princess and asked shyly, "Forgot what?"

"Oh! You talk!," said Princess happily.

"Yes," said the creature. "Of course I talk." She hesitated for a second. "You don't like eating baby opossums, do you?"

"What's a 'opossum?'"

"Well, we are!," said the Momma. Her babies clutched the fur on her back tightly and stared at Princess fearfully.

"OH!" Princess laughed. "No, I promise I won't eat your babies." She closed her eyes, shook her head, and placed a paw over her heart.

The Momma opossum exhaled in relief.

"I have food in a bowl in the kitchen." Princess gestured toward her cat door.

"You have food?!," asked the Momma, biting her lower lip.

"Yes, why? Are you hungry?"

"Very!," said the Momma, nodding her head quickly.

"Come on! Follow me!," said Princess. "You can eat from my bowl."

The momma opossum had never heard the word "bowl" before but she sensed that it had something to do with food, so she quickly followed the pretty blue-eyed creature.

"My name's Poopsie. What's your name?"

Princess couldn't help but giggle at little at the opossum's name, but she covered it up with a little cough.

"I'm Princess."

Up in the sky, a million miles away, the Wishing Star twinkled happily and beamed down at Princess. He was very proud of her for being kind to the strange-looking little family of opossums that he sent to her.

"And what are your babies' names?"

"Babies, tell Princess your names, please," said Poopsie.

"I'm ChooChoo," said one baby.

"I'm Petunia," said the baby girl opossum who was wearing a pretty purple petunia flower as a hat.

"I'm LeeLee." It came out very mumbled because she was sucking her thumb.

"I'm Lily," said the girl baby who was eating a lily flower.

"I'm Silly," said the baby who was giggling and hanging upside down on her back, holding onto her mother's fur with just her feet now.

"I'm Poppy!," another baby said as he popped up into the air from Poopsie's back and landed on top of little Silly, which caused her to giggle again.

"And I'm Sloppy!," said the last baby proudly. He had strawberry seeds stuck in the fur by his mouth and some mud and grass sticking to the fur on his head.

Princess giggled again.

Princess never forgot how awful it was to be lonely all the time. And she never forgot her promise to the Wishing Star to be kind. In return, Poopsie and her children and her children's children provided Princess with love and laughter and cherished friendships for the rest of her life.

Made in the USA
San Bernardino, CA
28 December 2016